MAVIS
BELFRAGE

A Romantic
Novel

With Five
Shorter Tales

London 1996

MAVIS
BELFRAGE

By
ALASDAIR GRAY

BLOOMSBURY

FIRST PUBLISHED IN 1996
BY BLOOMSBURY PUBLISHING PLC,
38 SOHO SQUARE, LONDON W1V 5DF
THIS PAPERBACK EDITION PUBLISHED 1997
COPYRIGHT © ALASDAIR GRAY 1996
THE MORAL RIGHT OF THE AUTHOR HAS BEEN
ASSERTED

"MONEY" FIRST APPEARED IN *SCOTLANDS,* 1994;
"EDISON'S *TRACTATUS*" IN *NEW NOVEL REVIEW*,
APRIL 1995; "THE SHORTEST TALE" IN *MADAM X,*
PUBLISHED BY COLOPHON, 1996.

TYPESET IN ZAPF HUMANIST
AND COURIER NEW BY
EM-DEE PRODUCTIONS, GLASGOW, SCOTLAND
DESIGNED & DECORATED BY ALASDAIR GRAY
PRINTED BY CLAYS LTD, ST IVES PLC, ENGLAND

A CIP CATALOGUE RECORD FOR THIS BOOK IS
AVAILABLE FROM THE BRITISH LIBRARY
INTERNATIONAL STANDARD BOOK NUMBER IS
0 7475 3089 0

FOR
ALEXANDRA GRAY
WHEN SHE IS
MUCH OLDER

TABLE OF

CONTENTS

MAVIS
BELFRAGE

PUBLICLY FUNDED LEARNING was once greatly valued in Britain. The minimum school leaving age had been raised to sixteen. New schools and colleges were built and old ones enlarged. Folk who would have missed university courses in other decades were helped to them by government grants. A solemn young Scot called Colin Kerr went to a famous South British university where he won a fairly good second class philosophy degree. This would have finished his education had he not met Mavis Belfrage.

1

He was lecturing in the teachers' training college of his native city. His students were nearly his own age but he thought them less intelligent. Some lecturers push ideas into listless brains by using forceful speech or by turning their classrooms into debating halls. Colin relied on repetition. He knew clever students found his method dull but thought he did most good by serving the majority. He also enjoyed putting complex ideas into simple, fluent sentences. During some monologues he was so hypnotized by the sound of his steady, quiet, distinct voice that he felt himself still at Cambridge.

One morning he spoke about what he called the Classical and Romantic theories of education, comparing teaching that strengthens a superior class by promoting obedience with teaching that strengthens individuals by suggesting a variety of choices. A distinct sigh and impatient movement interrupted him. It was not his habit to look straight at students but he knew their names and exactly where they sat. He said, "You seem restless Miss Belfrage. Do you want to say something?"

"No. I mean yes. What do you believe?"

"I'm sorry?"

"You've told us at great length how Plato and Rousseau disagree about what and why children should be taught. Who do you agree with?"

"I've no opinion."

"You must! It's your subject."

There was a general stir of interest. He ignored it by gazing thoughtfully at the ceiling and saying, "Of course I feel . . . flattered that an attractive young lady believes I can add something to the thoughts of Plato and Rousseau, but I know them better than you do. They were geniuses. Their ideas will exercise the minds of thinkers for centuries to come. The best I can do is explain them."

"That's a very *convenient* attitude for you, Mr Kerr, but not for *us*," said a sing-song Welsh voice from the back of the class. "You lecture *adults* on educational *theory* so need not choose between one theory and another. We will soon be managing classrooms of *children*. We will be *forced* to choose. I don't think Mavis wants you to choose for her. It's just that your lectures refuse to admit that choice is *necessary*. I think that sums it up?"

The voice belonged to Evans, a mature student who had sat beside Mavis Belfrage in that classroom, but not for a week or two.

"Your notion of choice is slightly absurd," said Colin with a touch of impatience. "What you eventually teach will be chosen for you by the Scottish curriculum council. How you teach will be decided by the school you are in and some character traits inherited from your parents – most of them based on self-esteem."

"That answers Mavis's question!" said the Welsh voice triumphantly. "If you think individual choice absurd you are a conforming Platonist."

"Wrong, Evans," said Colin cheerfully. "Plato thought educators should persuade people to conform. I am a pragmatic materialist who believes that even educators do as things do with them. But knowing this won't help anyone pass their end-of-term exam next week. My questions will be set on chapters two, five, nine and ten of Hoffman and MacKinlay's *Outline of Educational Theory*. Memorize these and you can forget all about me. Make a note of that, everyone – chapters two, five, nine and ten."

While most of the class scribbled in their notebooks he pretended not to see Mavis Belfrage sitting with folded arms and an ominous scowl.

"You will also get higher marks if you remember," he added, "that while I expect no one to show interest in my opinions, I have no interest at all in yours."

"Which is why you are such an uninspiring individ –" said Mavis sharply, then faltered and said " – lecturer."

The whole class stared from her to him. He removed his spectacles and stared thoughtfully back, wiping the lenses with a small oblong of yellow chamois leather. The faces of all but Mavis appeared featureless to him now. Perhaps emphatic lipstick and eyeshadow made her defiant glare unusually distinct. The glare stimulated him. He smiled, said, "Probably," and dismissed the class, pleased to have shown a fair-mindedness typical of Cambridge at its best.

A fortnight later he announced the exam results and asked Mavis Belfrage to visit his office in a free period of the following day.

2

Colin kept an office as impersonal as himself. One wall was the exact width of the door and two filing cabinets beside it. The cabinets had a row of text books and directories on top. The floor was just big enough for a desk with a chair before and behind it and a tin wastepaper basket. On the desk lay a phone, a clean glass ashtray for the use of visitors, a sheaf of pages covered with Mavis Belfrage's bold, irregular writing. The only wall decorations were a calendar and class timetable. The one colourful object was a small cube made of yellow and blue interlocking plastic bricks. Colin was attaching something like a propeller to this when his door was knocked firmly, once. He dropped the object in a drawer, and opened the door saying, "Come in Miss Belfrage. Please sit down."

"I won't be here long will I?" she asked, erect and facing him. She was black-haired, gaunt, the same height as him and dressed (he thought) more attractively than the day before. She stood with right hand in the pocket of a trousersuit, the other gripping the strap of a bag slung from her shoulder. To stop himself looking hard at her he sat down and waited. She sighed, sat across the desk from him, took cigarette and matchbook from her bag, lit the cigarette and tossed a match into his ashtray.

He said, "I want to talk about your exam paper."
"Yes. You want to apologize."
"No!" he said, surprised and amused, "certainly not. I know you dislike my teaching methods – during the past term you've made that obvious. But I respect your attitude and don't want you to think I gave you abnormally low marks out of bad feeling."
"But you did."
"No. Let us take your paper a question at a time."
He lifted the sheaf from the desk. She said swiftly, "No need. Did I write anything stupid in that paper?"
"No."
"Did I express myself badly?"
"You expressed your *self* magnificently."
"Did I show I understood the subject?"
"You showed that you thoroughly understand it."
"Yet you failed me."
"Yes. You did not answer my questions." (He examined the paper.) "I did not ask you to compare the ancient Greek, English public-school and American state education systems. I asked you to summarize Hoffman and MacKinlay's accounts of these systems. I don't pretend Hoffman and MacKinlay's account is the only intelligent account

possible. On most points I preferred yours. But I did not ask for yours. The whole class knew my questions would be based on Hoffman and MacKinlay. You knew it."

"Why are you terrified of your students' opinions?"

"They have nothing to do with me!" he said on a surprisingly petty note. Noticing this he blushed slightly. She stared at him then stubbed out her less than half smoked cigarette saying calmly, "I don't understand you but obviously you want me to think you're nothing but a conscientious, honest, decent, stupid bloke. All right, I believe it. Can I leave now?"

But it was he who stood up.

He went to the window, looked out and said, "How did you perform in your other subjects?"

"Surely you've heard about that from your colleagues?"

"Yes. Why did you do so badly?"

"For . . . personal reasons. For personal reasons my attendance has been poor. But I didn't do very badly. I was a borderline case. With reasonable marks in your subject I might just have scraped through. You marked me as low as possible."

"So you'll repeat the year?"

"I can't. They won't renew my grant."

She spoke in so low a voice that he looked at her. Her head was bowed. He said crisply, "I may be able to help."

She did not look up. He said, "If you're a borderline case I can explain to the Principal the special nature of your failure. If your reasons for poor attendance are not outrageous he might let you repeat a year. He's not a harsh man."

She shook her head and said, "There's no point.
You see, I can't stand children – not whole roomfuls
of them. Their problems bore me. Their manners
sicken me. That's why my attendance was bad, and
why I failed most of my practical tests. As for your
subject, I could have got high marks if I'd wanted
them but I decided to sink with flags flying and guns
firing instead of just . . . fading away. I suppose I did
it to annoy you. Sorry!"

She looked at him with a slightlt rueful but friendly
smile. He nodded and said, "What will you do now?"

"Find a job somewhere . . . I don't know."

"Can I take you out to dinner?"

"Why?" she asked, startled. He did not answer. She
said, "When?"

"Tomorrow night?"

She thought about that. "Thursday would be better."

"Will we meet in the lounge of the North British Hotel?
Say about seven?"

"Eight would be better."

"All right."

He went to the door and held it open saying, "Goodbye
Miss Belfrage."

She walked out past him saying, "Goodbye *Mister* Kerr."

He closed the door, smiling at the mockery she had
put into *Mister*. He was only comfortable with assertive
women and had met none of these socially since
leaving university.

3

Colin was ten minutes early for the meeting, Mavis Belfrage exactly on time. Each drank half a pint of lager in the lounge then shared a bottle of wine while dining in the restaurant. The invited woman mainly listened, the man who would pay for her mainly talked. He talked about Cambridge because he thought his life there more interesting than anything before or after; also because she seemed the sort of woman he had met at Cambridge. He told stories about dons, college servants and fellow students in a humorous, denigrating way which did not hide how much they had fascinated him. Mavis smiled and listened with an alertness which suggested she was trying to understand something behind his words. Wondering what it was he changed the subject to politics and was pleased when she began talking. She had left-wing radical views he thought sentimental in a woman with her expensive accent. He did not say so. Instead he described nuclear disarmament demonstrations he had marched with as a schoolboy, not mentioning that he had since become more conservative. When that topic was exhausted he was silent for a while, wondering how to get her talking about her own past. He ordered coffee and liqueurs then said abruptly, "What brought you to Scotland?"

"A man I once lived with came to work here."

"O?"

"Yes," she said, smiling at him.

"Em . . . Why did you stay here afterwards?"
"Scotland is as good a place as anywhere else."
Colin did not believe Scotland was as good a place as anywhere else. He suspected she was hiding something so changed the subject to avoid seeming suspicious.

"What are your plans for the future?"
"I never plan things," she said shaking her head. "I put up with them until they turn nasty then take the nearest way out. Just now I don't see any way out."
"That sounds serious. Why are you laughing?"
"Because I'm not a serious person and you obviously are!"
"I can't help it," he said, laughing too.
"You don't have to talk to me all the time, Colin. You're a sort I can enjoy being quiet with."
"That's a relief," he said thankfully, and watched while she sipped the liqueur and smoked a cigarette. He liked the elegant way she did these things.

The night was wet and windy when they left the hotel and she accepted his offer of a lift. From a city centre brightened by the fronts of big shops he drove to a district lit only by lamp posts and the glow from curtained tenement windows. He did not know this district. "Left at the next turning," and "Right now!" was all she said before telling him to stop at a kerb; then she turned to him and said, "Thank you Colin, I enjoyed this evening."
"Won't you ask me in for a coffee?"
In a harder but quieter voice she said, "Listen, if you insist on coming in with me you have to be very quiet.

The landlady hates my guts and is looking for an excuse to turn me out."

He nodded. They left the car. He closed the door carefully then followed her on tiptoe into the close of a tenement.

4

Two hours later they had made love and enjoyed it more than they had expected. Colin sat up in bed feeling better than he had ever felt before. He was astonished by how well he felt. Mavis seemed to be sleeping but without opening her eyes murmured, "You're quite a loverboy, aren't you?"

"You led me on."

"You let me. Some men can't."

"Have you had many men?"

"Have you had many women?"

He thought about two women he had once fucked with after a drunken party. It had been interesting but unsatisfying.

He said, "Let's not discuss that just now."

From the bedclothes under her chin a hand with pointing forefinger slid out. She aimed it at his heart murmuring, "You are being secretive because you've nothing to hide."

He laughed and agreed. Since his lively feelings needed an outlet he asked if he could make the cup of coffee he had asked for in the car.

"Yes, if you're quiet about it. There's water in the kettle."

"Can I put on some heat?"

"No. The gas is worked by a shilling meter and I'm out of shillings."

"I have a shilling."

"Keep it. The slot meter is in the hall and I don't want that nosy old bitch seeing you."

Amused by her English habit of calling a wee lobby *the hall* he said, "Will you put in the shilling? This room's freezing."

"No," (she snuggled deeper in the bedclothes) "I'm perfectly warm and cosy here."

He slipped on the overcoat he had hung over a bundle of garments on a hook behind the door. An electric kettle stood in the hearth of a boarded-up fireplace. The board was papered, as were the walls, with a pattern like red brickwork, its realism enhanced by patches of genuine damp and dirt. Mavis had hidden the brickwork as much as possible by pinning childish drawings over it and posters showing the faces of Che Guevara, James Dean and popular singers whose faces were as sullen as her own sometimes looked.

While waiting for the kettle to boil he said abruptly, "I'm afraid I need you."

"O I'm sorry!" she cried, staring at him.

"Why?"

She closed her eyes murmuring, "Nothing. It doesn't matter."

"I want you to live with me."

"O?"

"Will you live with me?"

"Why not? It will be convenient. I'm terribly short of money."

"Is that the only reason why you'll live with me?"

In a low voice she said, "No, Colin."

"You see I'd like us to get married."

"There's too much of that going on nowadays."

"I'd like it all the same."

"Why?"

"I prefer things to be conventional."

"I'm married already!" she said with a sudden smile of beautiful malicious glee. He shut his eyes for a moment then said, "When did you leave him?"

"Years ago."

"Was he bad to you?"

"No, he was nice. I only go for nice men."

"Why did you separate?"

"Because I'm a bit of a bitch."

"You're not a bitch!"

"Nice men never believe I'm a bitch."

The kettle boiled. He took it to a table by the bed where mugs and a jar of coffee powder stood among food tins and piles of magazines, mostly fashion magazines. While making the coffee something tugged at his mind. All the drawings on the wall showed big aeroplanes bombing tiny houses. He pointed to a heap of aeroplane magazines.

"Why are you fond of aeroplanes?"

"These belong to my son," she said, smiling sweetly.

"How old is he?"

"Eight."

"But!" cried Colin excitedly, "that means you're old! I mean, I'm sorry, older than me."

"Had you not noticed?" she asked coldly.

"No! I always think women who attract me are my own age or younger. Where is your son?"

"With a friend. He usually sleeps here."

"Where?" asked Colin looking round the tiny room.

"With me," she said taking a cigarette case from under her pillow.

"Is that healthy?"

"I honestly don't know. Give me that lighter."

"You've a horrible life Mavis," he said holding a flame to the tip of her cigarette. She looked at him across it and whispered, "Do you really want me?"

"I *need* you."

He removed her cigarette, kissed her then gave it back.

Then sat on the bed, warming his hands on the coffee mug and thinking hard.

"You'll be a lot happier with us," he said at last. "The lad can have a room of his own."

"Us?"

"My father and I. We took a house in Saint Leonard's Bank when I started at the college."

She looked uneasy so he assured her, "We're buying it through a decent building society. He pays a third and I pay two. I have the bigger salary, you see."

"What does your father do?"

"Keeps a hardware shop."

"So your posh accent isn't inherited."

"Acquired. I hope you don't mind."

"Will . . . your dad like me?"

"O yes, we never disagree about important things. I'll tell him tomorrow. But if you've no objection I'll come to bed again because I want to hold you again, just to make sure you're real."

5

At six thirty next morning he returned to Saint Leonard's Bank, a pleasant lane between a public park and a terrace of neat little Victorian houses with small front gardens. Colin entered his home quietly and quietly washed, shaved and changed his clothes. A morning paper was thrust through the letter-box. He took it to the kitchen and read while waiting for his father

who entered half an hour later saying, "Aye aye, out all night were we?"

"Yes. I must tell you about that."

"Son," said his father starting to make breakfast for them, "you don't need to tell me a thing."

"But I must tell you about this. I've met someone – a woman I'm keen on. I've asked her to stay with us."

"For the weekend?"

"For the foreseeable future."

"You want to marry her?" said his father, staring.

"Yes but I can't. She's married already and she has an eight-year-old son who'll stay with us too."

"Jesus Christ Almighty Colin! Have you got her into trouble?"

"I have not made her pregnant. I have no practical reason for wanting her."

"Who is she? What does she do?"

"She's called Mavis Belfrage, unemployed at present. She was a student of mine whose grant was cut because she failed her exams."

"So she has a practical reason for wanting you?"

"I've taken that into account. It doesn't matter."

"An eight-year-old son! She's no chicken, Colin."

"I've taken that into account."

His father, frowning, laid bacon rashers in a frying-pan. Colin lifted his paper and appeared to read.

"Listen!" said Mr Kerr a moment later, "when we took this house it was in my mind – and I thought in yours – that one day you'd meet a nice girl, marry, have weans and there would be room for us all here."

"That's right. What are you complaining about?"

"I never thought you'd pick up a family second hand!" said his father, chuckling. "Is it cheaper that way, Colin? Listen son, listen. You can do better for yourself. You don't need to take damaged goods."

Without raising his eyes from the newsprint Colin said quietly, "Keep your sales talk for the shop."

There was silence then he heard his father sigh and continue making breakfast. They ate without speaking.

6

Two days later Colin brought Mavis, her son and three suitcases to Saint Leonard's Bank and Mr Kerr welcomed them as warmly as Colin had expected.

"Come in come in come in!" he said. "Drop those cases. Here's where the coats go. The first thing you need in a new home is a nice cup of tea and something to eat."

He led them to the living-room.

"Wrong, Dad," said Colin, "the first thing we need is introductions. Mavis and Bill, this is Gordon my father. Gordon this is Mavis Belfrage and Bill Belfrage, her son."

"I can see why my Colin fell for you," said Gordon, smiling and shaking Mavis by the hand.

"Thank you."

"Hullo Bill Belfrage!" said Gordon, shaking the hand of a thin little boy who looked as unhappy as his mother and kept as close to her as possible. "Look around, Bill, and see if there's anything here you would like."

Bill looked furtively round the room. So did Mavis. Colin, trying to imagine it through her eyes, wondered if she thought it cheap and vulgar.

He had chosen the white walls, grey fitted carpet, Scandinavian furniture of blond wood and pale-grey upholstery. Colourful things came from the house where he had been born: curtains with repeat patterns of red-coated horsemen drinking stirrup-cups in the snowy yards of Tudor inns, a standard lamp with shade of scarlet pleated silk, bright brass and china ornaments on the sideboard and low bookcases. Before an electric wallfire stood an Indian brass-topped table set with tea things and a two-tiered stand holding plates of small triangular sandwiches and sweet biscuits. Between two china shepherdesses on the mantelpiece lay a long

cardboard box with a 1940 fighter plane depicted on
the side. This had held parts of a model Spitfire which, expertly assembled, now lay on top. After a quick glance at this Bill Belfrage looked away from it until Gordon said, "I thought a certain young man liked aeroplanes," and Mavis muttered, "Go and *look* at it Bill."

Bill walked to the fireplace and stood in front of the Spitfire.

"It's yours!" said Gordon.

"Say thanks," hissed Mavis.

"Thanks," muttered Bill and returned to her side.

"Colin's the one to thank," said Gordon. "He bought it for you."

"Thanks," Bill told Colin who murmured, "Don't mention it. I have lots of money."

"Well sit down sit down," said Gordon rubbing his hands together. "Tea Mavis?"

"To be frank . . . I can't stand tea."

"Coffee?"

"If it's no trouble."

"White, brown or black?"

"Whichever's the least trouble – I mean black."

"Sure you wouldn't like white?"

"Quite sure."

"What about you, Bill? Lemonade?"

Bill said, "Coffee. Black, please."

"Pull yourself together Bill," whispered Mavis.

"Lemonade then. No, tea. I can't stand lemonade."

"One black coffee and three teas coming up," said Gordon and left the room. No one had sat down.

Mavis turned to Colin and said, "I shouldn't be here."

"Yes you should."

"Why does your dad act as if the house is his when it's mostly yours?"

"Force of habit. He's trying to make you feel at home."

"I wish he would stop."

"You'll come to like him – he's a very good man."

She took the cigarette case from her shoulder bag, opened it, stared at a single cigarette and said, "God I'm nearly out."

"No, you're not," said Colin, taking a pack of twenty from his pocket and dropping it in her bag. She nodded, lit up, inhaled, exhaled then said pathetically, "Colin love me a little?"

He embraced her. She offered her mouth. Before their lips touched Bill shouted, "Mum! Come here!"

He had wandered to the end of the room and was out of sight round a corner. Mavis grimaced and went after him. Colin followed more slowly.

The room was L-shaped. Round a corner stood a dining-table upholding an architecture of small blue, yellow and white plastic bricks, a central part nearly touching the ceiling. The general form suggested a blend of Babylonian ziggurat, Roman Colosseum, Edinburgh Castle and Manhattan Island. Bill hurried round it stooping to keek through openings and standing on tiptoe to peer over barriers.

"What's this?" demanded Mavis.

"My hobby," said Colin meekly.

"What *is* it Colin?" asked Bill.

"It began as a city with a castle inside. I was so keen to make a really safe city that now most of the castle goes round the edge. It's not finished – I'm still working on it."

"You can't make a city safe nowadays!" cried Bill Belfrage scornfully. "One intercontinental ballistic missile will smash any castle in the world into little tiny radioactive bits."

"My city," said Colin regarding it with satisfaction, "is on a planet where they haven't learned to split the atom. They have no aeroplanes either. Or motor cars."

"Why isn't it finished?"

"I'm not satisfied by the position of the windmills."

Colin flicked a switch at the table edge. Little propellers began whirling on turret-tops round the outer walls.

"They look lovely!" cried Mavis. While surveying this large toy she had relaxed, become jaunty, was smoking now with total indifference to where the ash fell.

"They *look* all right," admitted Colin, "but a besieging army could destroy them with gunfire and then the city would lose light and heat. The windmills drive its generators."

He flicked another switch and light glowed behind a myriad of windows in the central towers.

"How can a planet have electricity without cars and aeroplanes?" cried Bill, shocked into indignation.

"You must work that out for yourself," said Colin, "but I'll give a clue. Their ships and locomotives are driven by wood-burning engines."

"Colin!" said Mavis softly. Laying hands on his shoulders she held him at arm's length, smiling with motherly humour. He looked back obstinately, ironically solemn.

"Get his mind off *that* nonsense, Mavis, and you'll do us all a favour," said Gordon carrying a large tea-pot and small coffee-pot to the table on the hearthrug.

"But I'm glad to find Colin has a touch of lunacy in him," she said, following Gordon and sitting on the sofa. "In everything else he's so abnormally safe and sober – unless you count his feeling for me."

"Now on *that* matter, for me to comment," said Gordon, grinning, "would be unbecoming to say the least. Have an ashtray."

He passed her a small blue china dish in which she automatically stubbed the half-smoked cigarette.

"Ready for your tea Bill?" said Gordon, sitting in an armchair and pouring coffee.

"In a minute," said Bill from the other end of the room.

The adults round the smaller table grew talkative. "When did Colin start building that thing Mr Kerr? It's huge."

"Call me Gordon, Mavis. It started when his mother and me gave him a box of Lego bricks on his eighth or ninth birthday. He made a clever little fort and kept tinkering with it so we gave him another box a year later. Of course in our old home he hadnae much room to expand. And, by the age of fourteen he had other interests and wouldnae have noticed if I'd broken the whole thing up and given it to Oxfam. I wish I had! Five months ago back he comes from Cambridge, brings the thing here and buys more boxes of Lego! He's worked on it during his free time ever since."

"Why?"

"He says Cambridge has spoiled him for social life in Scotland."

"It's true," said Colin. "The friends I had before I went south now meet in pubs I don't like and talk politics which don't interest me."

APPLIED
ECONOMY

"Who keeps the house so beautifully spotless and tidy?" said Mavis, looking about.

"We have a cleaning woman for an hour on Mondays and Fridays."

"Dad's being modest," said Colin. "He does practically everything. I'm no sort of housewife."

"Neither am I," said Mavis.

"I had to learn to be when Colin's mum passed away," said Gordon, smiling. "He was ten at the time and we hadnae the money to hire domestic help. But it's surprising what you can take satisfaction in when you apply yourself – even dusting a room."

"The application is what defeats me," said Mavis ruefully.

"Is there no oil on this planet of yours Colin?" asked Bill sitting down beside them and taking a biscuit.

"No fossil fuel of *any* kind."

"But they could have airships with steam-driven propellers."

"Not practical. Sparks from the furnace would ignite the gas and . . ."

"Not if they used helium. It's non-inflammable. I've looked into it."

"No steam engine could drive an airscrew fast enough to lift its weight."

"But if the airship was big enough –"

"The bigger the airship the more engines it needs. Early airships and aeroplanes were *equally* dependent on the petrol engine."

Bill sulked for a moment then shouted, "Rocket-powered gliders! What about them?"

"Listen Bill!" said Colin raising a warning finger, "if you mean to bomb my city you must expect me to defend it. I don't know how yet but I'll think of something – barrage balloons with gun platforms perhaps."

"That's all right," said Bill. Pointing to the Spitfire he added, "It's very nice but you ought to have let *me* fit it together."

"I meant to but got carried away."

"And now perhaps Bill would like tea?" suggested Gordon.

"Yes please," said Bill sprawling very low in an armchair with his hands in his pockets, "though it's only fair to tell you I take much more sugar than is healthy for a growing boy. Has your city a name, Colin?"

"Can't say. Never thought of one."

"You could call it Glonda. It's a name I've just invented."

7

As Mavis unpacked in the bedroom Colin said, "This is a bleak-looking room because I'm a natural Spartan. Change it how you want. Put up posters. Spread things around."

"But Gordon will come in and tidy it up."

"I've told him not to. This is our room and from now on he won't set foot here."

"Thanks but I want something else from you – a rent book."

"I'm not taking money from you!"

"I need it to prove to the Social Security office that I'm your lodger. If they know I'm fucking with you they'll cut my allowance."

"But you *will* be . . . cohabiting . . . with me. And I'll give you an allowance."

"In return for what? For housework? I don't want to encroach on your dad's territory. For fucking with you and you alone? That would be as bad as marrying again. Of course marriage is what you want – it's a game you've never played. I've played it. I don't like it. I need independence. Thank God I live in a country that will allow me some if I have a rent book and a landlord who signs it once a week."

"I'll give you a rent book," said Colin, sighing, "and even take your money, if you insist."

"I don't insist on *that*," she said, smiling. They were on the bed now, embracing. He said, "I hate lying to a public service but it won't be for long. You'll soon get a job."

"You don't realize how hard it is for me to find work. Women who interview me are always suspicious and men either have sex in mind and show it or try not to show it and act worse than the women. They all think they have the right to ask impertinent questions and I can't help showing how I despise that attitude."

"So you don't get a job."

"I don't get a job."

"Keep trying dear. It will make you less lonely while I'm at work and Bill is at school."

8

A fortnight later a community of three sat in the circle of rosy light cast by the standard lamp round the living-room fireplace. Mavis read a detective thriller. Bill sprawled on the hearthrug tracing pictures of aircraft from an illustrated book. Colin was altering a turret, replacing the propeller with a tiny spool. Beside him on the sofa a tray of turrets awaited the same treatment. Behind the sofa stood the big table supporting Glonda.

With stately steps Gordon arrived from the kitchen, flexing his arms and murmuring "aaaauch" like a man after worthwhile effort. Taking horn-rimmed spectacles from the mantelshelf he donned them, lifted a newspaper and settled in his chair to read.

"Gordon," said Mavis without looking up from her book, "you didn't need to wash the dishes."

"I don't mind washing a few dishes Mavis."

"I was going to do it later but after a meal I like to relax."

"Our difference is mibby due to early training," said Gordon amiably. "You can relax with dirty dishes near you. Not me! I've washed up automatically after meals for the last fourteen years. You cannae expect me to stop just because *you're* here."

"Good," said Mavis, glancing briefly at Colin who did not seem to notice. She went on reading. Gordon concentrated on his paper. Once his eyes rose when Mavis flicked ash far beyond the blue china ashtray

close to her hand but there was silence for several
minutes

      until turning a page he said, "Aye aye. I see
old Enoch is shooting his mouth off again."
"He's a menace," said Mavis sharply.
"A very clever man."
"The man's a menace."
Gordon smiled and laid the paper down with an air of
opening an interesting debate.
"Now there I don't agree. You, as an educated woman,
have to admit that Britain is overpopulated."
"The race issue has nothing to do with that. A third of
the immigrants into Britain are Irish. A third are whites
from Europe and our former colonies. Only a minority
are black or brown or yellow."
"I don't say Powell is right on the race issue; I *do* say
he's right on the immigration issue. Keep out the lot, I
say – Irish and ruddy Australians included."
"I wish you two were quieter," said Bill. "I find it hard
to concentrate."
"You forget that the British have been invading and
exploiting the countries of coloured people for well
over two centuries," said Mavis coldly. "We owe them
something back, I think."
"Who *haven't* the British upper classes exploited for
well over two centuries? My father was a docker in the
thirties, he could have told you about exploitation. It's
only since old Clement Attlee started breaking up the
ruddy old empire that the British worker has had a
decent livelihood and trade unions who can defend
him against the bosses. And now you upper-class

socialists lecture *us* on what *we* owe the coloured races!"

"I am NOT upper class!" said Mavis furiously stubbing out her cigarette.

"You've all the traits, Mavis."

"What traits?" she asked, glaring at him.

"Well the first that springs to mind is the way you smoke. You smoke all the time but never take more than a few puffs from each fag. If you'd known real poverty you'd smoke them to the tip like most folk do."

"What's the next trait that springs to mind?"

"Dad," said Colin quietly, "Bill is right. You're making too much noise."

"What's the next that springs to mind?" said Mavis as if Colin had not spoken.

"Nothing Mavis. I'm sorry," said Gordon in a low voice. He went on reading. So apparently did Mavis for a moment

then suddenly fired at Gordon with, "Do you know how much money Britain has invested overseas?"

"Sorry! Cannae help you there Mavis," he murmured, amused.

"Over a thousand million sterling: money bringing us wealth and goods without us giving back a thing to the third-world countries where it's invested. These investments don't just benefit the rich. Our tight little island floats nicely and evenly on a sea of dark-skinned poverty. And when some of the exploited climb aboard we scream that they're swamping us."

"You a Communist?"

"No."

"For someone who isnae a Communist you know a hell of a lot about British foreign investments," said Gordon with a hint of passion.

"Dad," said Colin. Gordon subsided

and two minutes later said cajolingly, "Mavis."

She did not look at him until he said, "Shall I tell you why I admire you? I admire you because you've opinions – strong ones – so you and I can have good brisk arguments with no holds barred. See my Colin? You couldnae start an argument with him if your life depended on it. He won't pass an opinion on a single thing."

Both Gordon and Mavis looked at Colin who carried the tray of turrets to his model city and began clipping them onto the walls. Bill sprang up and knelt on the sofa, watching.

"He used to have opinions," said Gordon. "He defended pacifism in his school debating society. When he was fourteen he marched to Aldermaston. He was the youngest member of a committee – what was it called? – The Committee of a Hundred. Him and me had some fine old argy-bargies in those days, because though I'm for the Labour Party I'm definitely moderate. Do you remember the arguments we had about that Colin?"

"Yes," said Colin drily.

"Then he went to university – Cambridge, no less. What did Cambridge do to you, Colin?

"Educated me."

"Look at him now! He won't voice an opinion. Doesn't

argue. Refuses to vote. And spends his spare time playing with toy bricks."

"I don't understand why people in this country think their opinions matter," murmured Colin, working on his city walls. "The Labour Party refuse to fight the stock exchange. The Tories refuse to fight the unions. The radical demonstrators link arms with the police and sing *Auld Lang Syne*. I refuse to feel angry about this. Like most of us I would hate a civil war with starvation, looting and machine-guns fired out of bedroom windows. Our political system is a means of using up energy which might change things. Political opinions are hobbies, like mine –" (he glanced with satisfaction at the towers of Glonda) "– exactly like mine."

"O!" cried Mavis flinging her book down, "I wish I could shake and shake you till you came *alive*!"

Colin looked at her with an obstinate little smile. Bill said plaintively, "Don't talk like that Mavis, it hurts my head. Colin, precisely when can I attack Glonda?"

"When it's complete."

"But you keep changing bits! I don't mind preparing an attack if I've a date to work toward but you won't give me one."

"Right. The fifth of November. Our war will start on the fifth of November. That gives us plenty of time."

"Don't depend on it Bill," said Mavis, "we may not be here by then. And now it's your bedtime."

She went on reading. The three males stared at her, Bill sullen, Gordon quizzical, Colin horrified. Gordon stood up saying, "How about hot chocolate and toast before you go Bill? *I'm* having some."

"All right," said Bill in a subdued voice. He gathered

his book and tracings, put them on the tea table and asked if he could leave them there till tomorrow. Neither Mavis nor Colin answered so he followed Gordon to the kitchen.

Colin sat on the sofa facing Mavis who looked brightly back. He said, "What's wrong?"
"I'm leaving, Colin. I came to live in your house – not your father's."
"Two thirds of it is mine!"
"Only legally."
"We . . . must talk about this later."
"Talk all you like. It won't change me."

9

At seven o'clock next morning Gordon, dressed for work, was boiling an egg in the kitchen when Colin, unshaven and morose, entered wearing dressing-gown and slippers. Gordon said, "Get yourself a mug – there's tea in the pot," and put another egg into simmering water.
"I'm tired," said Colin, yawning and pouring.
"I'm not surprised. The noise kept *me* awake till two thirty."
"What did you hear?"
"Nothing distinct – just a man and woman arguing."
"We'll have to leave, Dad," said Colin, sighing.
"Who's we?"
"Mavis, me and Bill. You see –"
"Don't explain!" said Gordon quickly. "Nothing needs

explaining. But *you're* not leaving. I can't pay for this house on my own you know."

"I'd still pay my share of it —"

"What! And the rent for somewhere else? And support a woman like Mavis?"

"I'll manage it," said Colin with obstinate calm. "Mavis has her Social Security allowance."

"She won't have it if the pair of you share the same lodgings. And how will I feel living alone in a house this size? All I need is a room and kitchen near the shop, Colin, somewhere with a decent pub round the corner. I've missed the pubs since we came out here."

Gordon performed deft movements which ended with him seated facing his son, a soft-boiled egg in a cup before each of them. Colin was watching him with a mournfulness Gordon seemed to find amusing.

"Stop looking tragic!" he cried. "You arenae driving a poor lonely old soul from hearth and home! I'm not fifty yet. I've more friends than you have. Anyway, I'll be here at weekends if only to weed the garden. I doubt if you or Mavis will do it."

"You're . . . a very . . . decent man," said Colin, smiling at him lovingly. Gordon grinned with pleasure then frowned and said, "Since I'm leaving I'll be so bold as to ask a question I couldnae have asked otherwise. Mavis. Why don't you boss her a bit? I think she'd be happier if you did."

"Boss her," said Colin, staring at his egg. "Taking orders is the thing she most hates. If I bossed her she would leave me."

"And you're afraid of that?"

"Terrified."

"Can't help you there son."

Gordon finished his breakfast and went to work. Colin returned to the curtained bedroom. Without switching on the light he sat on the bed beside Mavis and stroked her hair until she opened her eyes and said, "Mm?"
"I spoke to him."
"Well?"
"He's leaving."
She thought for a moment then said, "Won't that be very sad for him?"
"I think so. But he makes light of it."
"Well," said Mavis, yawning, "if you can accept it so can I. He isn't *my* father."

10

One Saturday Mavis returned to the house in Saint Leonard's Bank and found a cluster of toy balloons against the living-room ceiling. Strings hung from them. Colin and Bill were tying the ends to the turrets of Glonda.
"Hullo!" said Mavis dropping her shopping bag on a chair. "Have you noticed how late I am?"
Both had noticed. Colin had been worried but the sight of her made that irrelevant. He had never seen her so cheerful. He sat down to enjoy the sight, stretching his arms and saying, "It doesn't matter. I gave Bill his tea."
"I knew you would."
With dance-like movements she went to the window

and rearranged flowers in a vase saying, "I met Clive Evans in the supermarket. It was nice meeting an old friend. He took me for a meal."

"Evans the Welshman?" asked Colin, still contemplating her with pleasure.

"Yes. It was fun meeting him by accident like that. He's teaching now. Do I seem drunk?"

"You seem cheerful. He bought you a drink?"

"No, he admired me. I made a tremendous impression on him. Don't *you* feel intoxicated when someone admires you?"

"People don't admire me," said Colin smiling ruefully.

"Make them! It should be easy. You're full of good qualities. Bill you scruffy little tyke, let me have a look at you."

Bill was still tying balloon strings to spools on the sides of turrets. She pressed his head forward, peered at the nape of his neck and said, "A bath is what you need, my lad. Upstairs, undress and get into one. Scoot!"

"I had a bath last night, Mavis."

"You need another. Scoot!"

Bill pulled a face and left. Colin said thoughtfully, "I never liked Evans. Did you?"

"In college? O no. He was pompous and smug. Do you remember how he said 'I think that sums it up?' whenever he thought he'd been smart? But outside college he's different, very witty and funny. Almost as big a surprise as you."

"In what way?"

"In college you were suave, aloof, dominating. Outside you were mothered by your daddy and play with toys on the living-room table."

Colin brooded on this until she sat by him and leant
against his side, then he relaxed, sighed and murmured,
"Well, you're happy Mavis. That's good."
In a childish, confiding voice she said, "I want to ask
you a favour."
"Mm?"
"But first you must promise not to be angry."
"Why should I be angry?"
"I can't possibly tell you until you promise not to be."
"All right. I promise."
She held his hand palm upward and stroked the lines
on it with her forefinger saying slowly, "Colin, Clive –
Clive Evans I mean – would like an affair with me and
I would love one with him –"
He pulled his hand away; she cried, "You promised
not to be angry!"

He stood, stepped away, turned and saw her lying
back in the sofa watching him alertly. He said, "You
want to leave me?"
"No, I . . . I think I love you Colin. You're the decentest
man I know, besides being my only friend. But I'll leave
if you like."
"Why? What's wrong with us?"
"Frankly the sex thing isn't the fun it used to be, is it?"
"Isn't it?"
"You know it's not. You're still very sweet and tender
of course but you leave all the work to *me*."
"You said you dislike assertive men."
"I do but there should be a middle way . . . Don't look
so miserable Colin!"
She rose and came to him saying, "Listen, order me

not to do it. Tell me not to see him and maybe I won't."

"I can't *order* you to do anything," he told her grimly. "We aren't married. We've made no promises. You can leave me when you like. I can ask you to leave when I like."

"Are you asking me to leave?"

"No," he said and turned away feeling cold, hard and defeated. "I need you."

"And you're not angry?"

"Do you care how I feel?"

"You haven't scrubbed my back for *years* Mavis," said Bill querulously. He stood in the doorway, barefoot and in his dressing-gown. Mavis said, "Get into the bath, I'll be with you in a minute."

Bill left and Colin said firmly, "Bill must not know about this. If he finds out you must both leave here at once. I mean that, Mavis."

"Of course Bill won't find out. I'll tell him I'm going to evening classes and I'll always be home long before breakfast. O don't look sad! I feel so happy and hopeful. I wish I could put half my good feelings into you, Colin." He could think of nothing to say. From sounding wistful and cajoling she became brisk and sensible.

"I suppose you've a hot meal in the oven?"

"Casserole for two," he said bitterly.

"I bought us a bottle of wine. I'll see to Bill and be down in half an hour. I'm not as hungry as you of course, but we'll still have a nice meal and a quiet evening together and you'll soon see everything in its proper perspective. Don't worry. Nothing dreadful is happening to us."

But Colin thought it was.

When she returned from upstairs she served the
meal, poured wine and played Scrabble afterward, treating him with gentle, unfamiliar tact which made him want to cling to her whenever he forgot the horrid reason for it. He won the game by over two hundred points. She chuckled and said, "That's a healthy sign."

"What's a healthy sign?"

"You usually make me win by deliberately playing badly in the last fifteen minutes."

He smiled slightly and said, "I thought you hadn't noticed."

"I enjoy winning but I'm not stupid. Come to bed, Colin." She got up and kissed the top of his head.

"In a while."

He sat by the living-room fire wondering how to share the bed with her and respect himself. He also wondered what would happen if he ordered her not to see Evans as she had suggested, but the result seemed obvious: she would pretend to submit and deceive him.

"Don't make a liar of her," he told himself. "That would be even worse."

When he went to the bedroom at half past two she was sound asleep. He undressed quietly in the dark, slid between the sheets and lay apart from her. A little later she rolled without waking into the gap between them, pressed her length against him and embraced him with an inarticulate murmur like the purr of a cat. He had no will to pull away from his only source of comfort. He hoped the instinctive acts of a sleeping woman meant more than the conscious acts of a waking one. He hoped so for a long time before falling asleep.

11

He passed the next day in a numbness which she treated with the quiet efficiency of a good mother attending a convalescent child. She gave him breakfast and the Sunday papers in bed and later ran water for his bath. The weather was pleasantly mild so she suggested a visit to the seaside. He did not reject the idea. She made a picnic lunch and drove them to a long lonely beach approached by a farm track. They found a sheltered hollow and sat reading the Sunday papers while Bill floated driftwood in pools, combed the beach for shells and flotsam, used a stick to engrave huge aeroplanes and airships on smooth sand. When they returned home Mavis made an evening meal with deft rapidity, put Bill to bed at his usual hour, read him a story (which was usually Colin's job) then drove off in the car.

Colin heard it return as he lay on his back staring at darkness. He had lain like that since going to bed and intended to act as if sleeping when she entered the room. Misery made him less stoical. She entered softly and switched on a bedside lamp. He did not move but stared at the yellow circle cast by the lamp on the ceiling. He heard her undress and say gently, "Hullo Colin. You should be asleep. It's nearly four."
He did not move. He felt the mattress dip as she sat on the edge and asked sympathetically, "Are you very miserable?"
He did not move.

"Am I hurting you a lot? Am I being wicked?"
There was fear in her voice. She fumbled under the bedclothes for his hand and grasped it pleading, "Colin please tell me I'm not wicked!"

He said wearily, "It's all right Mavis."
She caressed his face crying, "Yes it *is* all right isn't it Colin? Make me believe it's all right, make me believe it."
Roused by her greater need he sat up and cuddled her saying, "Don't worry Mavis, you're beautiful, you're a queen. Queens don't need to care. Queens can do what they like."
Panic-stricken she commanded, "Say that again Colin! Make me believe it! *Make* me believe it!"
She grabbed him, clawing so desperately that pain made him grip her wrists and use the weight of his body to control her. Their fucking became mutual rape. After it they lay back to back and again he felt cold, hard and defeated. He wondered bitterly, "Is that what she enjoys doing with Clive Evans? Will she give him up now she can do it with me?"

But two nights later she visited Evans again.

12

Colin Kerr usually found his college work a dull business but now it started giving him moments of peaceful happiness, moments when he forgot Mavis Belfrage. He could not forget her at home. On nights when she was away the pain of remembering made sleep impossible. On the third such night he got up two hours after going to bed. In dressing-gown and slippers he filled a Thermos jug with hot milky tea, carried it with a mug to the living-room, put them on the mantelshelf and strolled morosely round the city of Glonda. It was dusty from neglect. Balloons, wrinkled from loss of gas, lolled between towers or dangled by their strings from the edge. Stretching across to the central tower he detached the upper half and placed it on the fireside table. For a few minutes he sipped a mug of tea while contemplating it, then sat down and made changes which would crown it with a revolving gun platform.

A while later someone said, "Do you think that's an improvement?"

Bill, also in dressing-gown and slippers, stood nearby watching. Colin frowned at his handiwork then muttered, "Yes I do. Why aren't you sleeping?"

"Nobody can sleep *every* night of the year."

"I suppose not."

"This is the first time you've touched Glonda since we added the balloons."

"Yes, I've had other things on my mind. Please go back to bed."

"That tower will collapse if an enemy as much as whistles at it."

Springing up from the sofa Colin screamed, "*Leave me alone! Get to bed will you?*"

Bill's pale face grew slightly paler but his expression did not change. Without moving he said, "I worry too when she's out all night."

Colin stared at him. Bill said, "I know it's depressing

but one develops a certain tolerance."

"Have some tea Bill," said Colin. He filled his empty mug and handed it over. They sat side by side, the boy sipping and watching while the man deftly completed his tower, carried it to the table and fixed it in place.

"Our war plans have been languishing for some time," said Bill.

"Yes, I really have had a lot on my mind."

"Well is there any *point* in waiting for the fifth of November? That's what I want to know."

Colin folded his arms, considered Glonda then said quietly, "You're right. There's no point in waiting. We'll destroy it now."

"We? Aren't you going to defend it?"

"Not me," said Colin pacing round the walls. "This is an evil city which has grown great by conquering weaker people outside. But now she has sunk into decadence and corruption. Her defences are neglected. Her balloons are out of gas. This is our opportunity."

"Who are we?"

"Brilliant but neglected scientists who belong to the exploited outsiders. Carefully, in the secrecy of an abandoned coalmine, we have invented and constructed two aeroplanes. Take this one."

A recently assembled model Messerschmitt lay beside the Spitfire on the bookcase. Bill took the Messerschmitt grumbling, "There's no oil on this planet."

"None, but the engines of these planes are fuelled by alcohol – distilled spirit – a discovery which only a genius like *you*, Herr Professor Bill Belfrage, could possibly have hit upon."

"I think *someone* ought to defend the city," said Bill

though Colin's purposeful manner had begun to excite him.

"Our planes can carry only one bomb at a time," said Colin taking books from the shelves and carrying them to a corner, "and since we have only managed to make six of them each bomb must be made to do the maximum damage. We must circle the entire city while picking our target and choose it carefully. I will strike from the north . . ." (Colin laid down three books with the Spitfire on top then strode to the diagonally opposite corner) ". . . you will strike from the south."

"Are three bombs each enough?"

"*Your* three will be enough. I am giving you Plato, Rousseau, and the most potent explosive known to mankind – Hoffman and MacKinlay's *Outline of Educational Theory*. Down on your knees man! Remain in hiding until you receive my signal."

Bill, trembling with excitement, knelt in the corner with book in one hand and Messerschmitt in the other. Colin went to the window, pulled back the curtains and looked out. In dark-grey light the tiny garden was still indistinct. He looked at his watch and sighed

then turned to the room and said quietly, "Twenty past six. Dawn has not yet broken over the doomed city's final day as, weakened by a night of debauchery, she writhes in uneasy slumber. But from beyond the horizon (get ready for your first flight Bill) from beyond the southern horizon there slowly rises –"

"Let's have music like in the pictures!" shouted Bill.

"Good idea," said Colin. He went to the radiogram
and looked along a stand of records murmuring, "Holst's *Planets* Suite? Trite. Wagner? Equally trite. Why should destruction be sombre and strenuous? It is building and keeping things up which is strenuous. Destruction should be gay, don't you agree Bill? All things built get knocked down again and those who knock them down are gay."

"Hurry up with it!"

Colin fitted a disc onto the turntable, set it turning and after a couple of trials held the end of the arm above the groove he wanted. He said, "I'll provide the commentary. Don't drop your first bomb before the music starts, then I'll drop the next bomb. Where was I?"

"The debauchery bit."

"Weakened by debauchery Glonda writhes in uneasy slumber until gradually, from beyond the southern horizon, there slowly rises, very slowly Bill, the hitherto undreamed of shape of a deadly aircraft, the first this planet has ever seen! Warily it approaches the fortress city and circles her titanic battlements. A few sleepy sentries observe with wonder as she carefully selects her target. Have you done that? –"

"Yes –"

"BLITZKRIEG!"

Colin lowered the needle into Handel's Hallelujah Chorus. Bill, stalking round the big table on tiptoe holding his plane as high as possible, threw with the other hand a book which rebounded harmlessly from the central tower. Colin rushed to the other corner, lifted a volume with both hands and hurled it with an accuracy which brought down the central tower and several others.

"You aren't using your plane!" screamed Bill.

"In this phase of warfare all rules are abandoned!" cried Colin shying two more books which destroyed great sections of wall and burst some balloons.

"Then I'm getting more bombs!" screamed Bill, hurling the remaining two and rushing to the shelves.

"Throw them spine first you idiot!" roared Colin.

"I'm NOT an idiot! You're the idiot!" screamed Bill. Taking a heavy atlas he walked round the table, deliberately using the spine to hammer down anything that stood up. He was sobbing breathlessly, Colin thought from exertion, until Bill dropped the atlas, sat down, hid face in hands and wept. Colin realized Bill was sorry Glonda had been destroyed. He switched the record off and went to him across a carpet scattered with blue, yellow and white wreckage.

"Sorry Bill," he said, sighing and patting the boy's shoulder, "sorry about that."

Bill became as silent as if he too had been switched off. Mavis was in the room.

She stood with hand on hip, the other gripping the strap of her shoulder bag, on her face the look of a disapproving schoolmistress. She said, "What are you two crazy infants playing at?"

"War games," said Colin.

"I'm not surprised at anything *you* do Colin but I thought Bill had some self-control."

"I couldn't sleep either," said Bill.

"Hm! And now I suppose you both expect me to

make a great big breakfast. All right. I will."
She went to the kitchen.
"She's not angry with us," Bill assured Colin in a whisper before following her. After a while Colin followed too.

13

The males sat side by side at the kitchen table while Mavis made omelettes. Bill said, "Will you build another city to knock down?"
"No. It takes too long."
"What will we do now?"
"I'll have to think about that."
"Do you know what our trouble is Colin Kerr?" said Mavis. "We don't have enough fun together."
"I'm bad at fun."
"Well I'm going to teach you to be good at it. We're going to have a party."
"What a great idea!" shouted Bill. She said, "Don't fool yourself Bill Belfrage. This party will only start when *you* are tucked up in bed."
"A party," said Colin, pondering.
"Yes. You must have friends, Colin."
"I have friendly acquaintances – colleagues, mostly."
"Invite them and we'll make them drunk on doped whisky. Dull people can be quite entertaining when they're drunk."
"A very bad idea."
"I was *joking* Colin! But I know how to make an innocent-tasting punch with a kick like a mule. And

what about your father?" she asked, setting plates before them. "I bet Gordon knows how to enjoy a party. And there's Clive – Clive Evans, you know."

She sat facing him. He stared at her. She nodded back and said, "He's great fun – socially I mean. You'll like him."

"*You'll* let me come to the party Colin? Please Colin?" Bill pleaded.

"No!" snapped Colin. He laid down the cutlery and shut his eyes feeling too tired to think or speak. He heard Bill mutter, "I had *almost* decided to regard you as a friend, but you act like a friendly sea-lion with unexpectedly vicious traits."

He heard Mavis say, "It's strange that you and I have never been to a party together, Colin. I used to go to so many."

He felt her hand touch his, despised himself for the comfort this gave yet relaxed for a quarter minute into something like sleep

                    then wakened and quickly breakfasted because he must wash and dress for work. As he ate she suggested it should be a dinner party for ten – she could easily make a meal for ten – all Colin need do was ask his father and any six others he liked one Saturday evening a fortnight hence. That would give her plenty of time to prepare. Colin neither objected nor agreed to these suggestions but when he left the table she obviously thought the matter settled.

14

A week passed before Colin asked his father and some other people to the party. Mavis no longer went out at night. Perhaps she met Evans during the day. Since Evans had a job this could only be during his lunch hour, so the nature of her affair had changed and Colin hoped it was maybe dying of natural causes. The party would show colleagues that he and Mavis were living as husband and wife. The Welshman would see this too so when Evans left the party with the other guests his affair with Mavis could decently end. Colin considered suggesting this to Mavis but decided against making a selfish remark while she worked so hard to make him happy. As the party neared she grew more and more domestic, cleaning and tidying the house as his father had done, beautifying it with flowers and candles as his mother had never done. The Kerr candlesticks had been for decoration only but Mavis used them to light the dining-table which had once supported Glonda. Each night she placed there a different, surprisingly tasty meal. Colin showed appreciation by doubling her housekeeping allowance.

"I suppose I deserve it," she said, kissing him. He decided he need fear nothing from Evans and persuaded Mavis to let Bill stay up for the meal if he went to bed immediately after.

On Saturday afternoon Colin drove into town with a shopping list written by Mavis for more wines and spirits than he thought necessary. She had made him promise not to come home before five because that would spoil a surprise she was preparing. He guessed the surprise would be something she wore so decided to surprise her back. Visiting a gentleman's outfitter he changed his dark pullover and knitted tie for a red waistcoat and scarlet silk cravat. When he entered the living-room she laughed and said, "You peacock, you've outdone me."

"O no," said Colin, staring at her. She looked dazzling in white silk pants and white velvet tunic patterned with seed pearls, silver beads and minute mirrors.

"That must have . . . cost . . . a lot," he said hesitantly.

"If you mean did I buy them out of my earnings as a street-walker the answer is *no*. You've never seen all the treasures packed in the cases I drag from lodging to lodging, Colin Kerr!"

"What's a street-walker?" asked Bill looking up from a comic he was reading. He too was sprucely dressed with well-polished shoes and neatly combed hair.

"I'll tell you one day when Colin isn't here – Colin's easily embarrassed. But Colin, look around! Isn't the room lovely? Doesn't the dining-table look inviting? Won't your colleagues envy you for having such an efficient, loving, beautifully dressed, beautiful mistress?"

Colin nibbled a nut from a dish of them on the bookcase and said, "Yes there dawns on me, waveringly, the notion that I will enjoy this party."

"Of course you will, and Colin!" (she laid a hand on his shoulder and looked at him with a girlish little pout) "I've a favour to ask – why are you grinning?"

"When you're extra cheerful then ask me a favour it's usually for something I hate to do."

"Is there anything you wouldn't do for me?"
"Probably not."
She put her hands behind her back and said slowly,
"Well I thought you, me and Bill would have a nice
little snack together just now, and after that you might
drive over to Comely Park which is where Clive – Clive
Evans – lives and bring him back. You see he hasn't a
car, this place is hard to find by bus and . . . well there
would be time for the two of you to go to a pub and
have a pint together – before the other guests arrive, I
mean. But of course you needn't have a drink with
him if you don't feel like one. But I think you'd enjoy
his company."
"No," said Colin.
"What do you mean?"
"I won't go."
"Why not?"
"Bill," said Colin, "Mavis is going to make us a snack.
Wash your hands please."
"Are you two going to have a boring emotional
storm?"
"Get lost Bill," said Mavis. Bill pulled a face and went
out leaving Colin and Mavis facing each other.

In a dangerously quiet voice she again asked Colin
why he would not go. He replied in a voice which in
his own ears sounded absurdly rational and laborious.
"Mavis, I do not dislike Evans because he is your
lover. In that he has my sympathy because I would
like to be your lover. And it isn't impossible for me to
meet him at a party and say the meaningless things
people say to each other at parties. But I refuse to

treat him as a friend to satisfy either your vanity or convenience."

"What a small tiny shrivelled ungenerous . . ." (she paused and grinned mockingly) ". . . *mind* you have!"

He stared back at her and then sat down. She walked forward and back saying, "What do you suggest I do? I've told him to expect you. What do you suggest I do?"

"Phone him and tell him to come by taxi."

"You do it. It's your idea – not mine."

"No."

He employed his agitation by picking up Bill's comic and staring at it blindly. After a few more aimless steps Mavis folded her arms and said, "I'll explain why I arranged for you to pick him up. He didn't *want* to come to this bloody party. He thought you would hate him because of me. I told him you were above such petty feelings. I said you would prove it by giving him a lift."

In a very low voice Colin said this showed that Evans understood and respected his feelings more than Mavis did; she should phone Evans, tell him she had been wrong and apologize. She flushed red and cried, "Phone him and tell him I'm . . ! What about the party? What sort of time will I have here without Clive, with only you and your friends and your father to talk to? Nobody kind? Nobody who loves me?"

"Our guests," he said with hard clarity, "will be decent, reasonable men and women."

"Unlike me, you mean. Tell them I may be rather late as I've gone to pick up a friend. There's a piece of meat in the oven. It will be ready by eight if you don't burn it."

She strode to the door. He jumped up crying, "If you

take the car you'll have plenty of time to get back before
the guests arrive!"

"I'll certainly take the car," she said and left.

Half a minute after the front door was slammed
Colin heard Bill say, "I suppose I can come back now
that people have stopped shouting. Have you a pain
there?"
Colin, looking down, noticed his hand was pressing
his midriff and was surprised to feel tension there. He
nodded.
"It goes away when she comes back," Bill told him.
"Will we look at the meat?"
But Colin knew nothing about serving a complex meal.
He phoned his father and asked him to come earlier
to help with an unexpected snag, then he went upstairs
and changed his clothes for less festive ones.

15

Gordon was the only guest who did not find the party
perplexing. The rest expected Colin to be less taciturn
than at college but between short spasms of small talk
he was more so. He had not told them he was living
with a woman yet the place had a feminine look. His
father (who they met for the first time) served the meal
with eager assistance from a small boy who said he
was Bill Belfrage and that his mother had gone to fetch
a friend and would turn up eventually.
"Her movements are sometimes slightly erratic," he
explained.

"Bill Belfrage!" said Doctor Schweik thoughtfully. "In my psychology class last term I had a student called Mavis Belfrage. Your mother perhaps?"

"Yes!"

"A good-looking woman who asked interesting questions but, as you say, was a little erratic. Who has she gone to fetch?"

Bill looked at Colin who seemed listening for a sound outside the room. Schweik repeated his question. Colin said, "I think he's called Evans."

"Evans? Clive Evans? He used to sit beside Mavis in my psychology class and he too asked interesting questions. I look forward to meeting them once more."

The other guests knew each other almost as little as they knew Colin. Schweik became the star of the party because he could talk with little or no help from others. After the meal three guests gave reasons for leaving early, the rest gathered near the fire. Bill, refusing to go to bed, dozed on an armchair with his hands in his pockets.

"For years no one has been a more radical critic of the system than myself," said Schweik, "but an extended bureaucracy is no answer to the problems created by a bureaucracy."

"I'm glad you said that. It so definitely did need saying," said another lecturer who was inclined to fawn on Schweik.

"That was a lovely piece of meat Colin," said the other lecturer's wife.

"These ego-powered rebellions change a few superficial details and leave us with even more unwieldy superstructures," said Schweik. "Colin will agree with me."

"I'm trying to keep an open mind," said Colin.

"Do you see a solution?" asked the other lecturer.

"None, because I see no problem. Our societies are shaped by technological evolution, the only effective historical manifestation of the human will when religion fails. Since the shaping process is often painful many feel compelled to exclaim and proclaim and campaign, especially in democracies where crushed worms are permitted to wriggle. But nobody is being badly crushed in comfortable little Britain where the Labour Party draws its strength from the support of the trade unions."

"Do you know what you're talking about?" asked Gordon who was listening with an obvious mixture of amusement, boredom and exasperation.

"Unfortunately yes. And now I regret I can stay no longer," said Schweik glancing at his wristwatch. "It is a pity. I would have liked to meet charming Mavis again. One remembers interesting students because the majority are dead timber, psychologically speaking."

"So why teach them psychology?" asked Gordon.

"Ah Mr Kerr, we academics are entitled to question everyone but our paymasters!" said Schweik smiling and standing up. "May I offer you a lift into town Mr Kerr?"

"Very kind of you. Yes, you may. The last bus went twenty minutes ago."

The guests left and Colin gently shook Bill awake saying, "Go upstairs Bill. I'll wait for her."

"Pull yourself together," said Bill, yawning. "Things aren't as bad as you think."

He wandered off to bed. Colin waited.

At half past three she came home and looked into the living-room with the cool sympathy of a surgeon visiting a patient after an operation.

"Hullo," she said.

"Hullo."

"How did it go?"

"Can't you guess?"

"Yes. I suppose that's what frightened me away. You're brooding. You should be in bed."

He neither moved nor looked at her. She said, "If you want me to apologize I will. I'll even try to be abject. Will I apologize?"

"No."

"Then I may as well go to bed myself."

On a gentler note she added, "Come to bed Colin. I'll be nice to you. You know I can be, sometimes."

"No."

"Well, good night. I ought to feel guilty but I've worn that feeling out. I told you I was a bitch at the very start, Colin."

"Can you not *change*, Mavis?"

"O yes. One day I'll be old and lonely because nobody will find me attractive. Meanwhile you must either kick me out or let me stay. Brooding can't alter that."

"It must."

"Well, Colin, if you think of something don't wake me with it. I'm very tired."

She went to bed and he continued thinking hard. The problem was that he could not sleep without her and could not join her in bed without loathing himself.

16

He wakened her at eighteen minutes past six, switching on the bedside light, sitting on the mattress edge and saying eagerly, "I know what to do, Mavis! I know what to do!"

Dazed and puzzled she opened her eyes saying, "What's happening?"

"Nothing. I've just worked out what to do. You see, you hurt and humiliated me tonight, publicly, without needing to. I won't be able to rest until I've hurt you back."

With open right hand he smacked her on one cheek, with open left hand hit the other, then lay beside her watching the result. Since she neither cried nor winced the pain may not have been great. Her bewildered look did not change until suddenly blushing red all over she scrambled out of bed away from him, staring and stammering faintly, "You . . ! You . . !"

She seized a hairbrush from the dressing-table and raised it defensively or threateningly, he could not say which but assured her, "I'm all right now. We're even. Now I can rest."

She thrust her face close to his and asked in a quiet, breathless voice, "Happy are you?"

"No."

"Never mind. You've beaten a woman. You must think yourself a real he-man."

"No, but now I'm able to sleep."

"Never mind. It'll do your ego a power of good."

Thrusting her face close to his she yelled, "Would you like to do it again?"

"Twice was enough."

She sneered, scooped clothes from a chair and went to the door. He sighed and said patiently, "Come back to bed Mavis."

She spat at him and went out.

He lay listening to her rouse and dress an unwilling Bill Belfrage and order him downstairs. She returned to the bedroom and, ignoring his remark that all this fuss was needless, took several things from the wardrobe and went downstairs. Colin arose and followed. Dressed for outdoors she knelt on a bulging suitcase on the lobby floor, tightening straps and watched by Bill who was similarly dressed.

"Where are we going Mavis?" Bill asked querulously.

She did not answer. Colin said, "You can tell him – I won't hound you."

Through clenched teeth she muttered, "I don't know where we're going."

"Stay here till you do," said Colin. "Sleep in Gordon's old room if you've finished with me."

She picked up the suitcase and told Bill, "Open the front door."

Bill did.

"Mavis," said Colin, "borrow my car but I want it back – tomorrow night, if possible."

"I'm not a thief, don't worry," she muttered.

"Goodbye," said Colin.

"Say goodbye," she commanded Bill.

"Goodbye," said Bill.

The door closed behind mother and son and that was the last time Colin Kerr saw Bill Belfrage.

17

He heard the car returning soon after eleven on Monday morning. He heard her enter the front door and climb the stairs. She came into the bedroom carrying a suitcase, went straight to the dressing-table, opened the top drawer and half emptied it before noticing him in bed watching her. Startled she said, "Hullo! Why are you not at work?"

He did not answer. Partly amused, partly disdainful she looked at a glass and half-full vodka bottle on the bedside table and asked, "Are you drinking?"

"Yes," he said thickly. "Don't like it much."

"Then stop it. You'd better phone Gordon as soon as possible. I'm here to clear out the last of my things and leave the keys and the car."

She finished packing then sat for a moment not looking at him, twisting her fingers together and saying, "Colin I'm not angry that you hit me, please don't think that. I'm surprised now you didn't do it sooner. But we've become bad for each other, very bad, I don't know why. We'd better not meet again. I also think you should send for your father. You need company – someone to look after you – but there's clean socks and underwear here which should last a fortnight."

He said loudly, "I don't want, in a day, or a week, or a fortnight, to find in a drawer the socks you cleaned and folded up for me yesterday morning when we were both happy."

"Well, I think you should very soon get in touch with Gordon. There – I've put the keys in this little dish.

Goodbye."

"Mavis!" he cried, heaving himself up a little on an elbow and blinking at her. She paused in the doorway, watching him in a haunted way. His thick, clogged voice tried to reassure her.

"Mavis whatever happens don worry. Good things don go bad because they nevr last. Y're all right Mavis. Whatever happens evything right. Member that!"

She hurried away and he heard the front door shut

and shortly after got up, pulled a dressing-gown over his pyjamas, took a pillow from the bed and carried it down to the kitchen. Here he slightly scorched his fingers removing a metal cap covering a pilot light on the cooker. Stooping he managed, after several efforts, to blow the light out. Opening the oven door he removed two sliding grids, put the pillow inside, turned the oven burners full on then lay on the kitchen floor with head on the pillow breathing deeply. He breathed deeply for what seemed several minutes then wondered why the only alteration to mind and body seemed a greater sobriety. When small he had heard his mother's friends whisper solemnly, "she put her head in the gas oven", "they put their heads in the gas oven", so had thought gassing a swift and simple way to die, but of course gossip always simplifies things. He tried to consider the matter scientifically. If coal gas was lighter than air it was flowing up to the kitchen ceiling, so would not suffocate him until enough had collected to fill the room down to the level of his nostrils. If heavier than air it

was pouring past him onto the kitchen floor and would
only work when it had risen upward to cover him like water. Should he stand up and start again by covering the oven with a tent of hanging blankets and crawling under? But perhaps the prospect of death had so speeded his thinking that what now seemed ten minutes was only a few seconds. At that moment he heard the front door open. Gordon was now the only other person with a key to it. With Keystone Cops rapidity Colin jumped up from the floor, switched off the oven, snatched out the pillow, closed the cooker door.

Gordon entered the kitchen and found his son sitting at the table with folded arms on a pillow. Colin said, "Hullo Dad."
"What's wrong with you? Why's your phone off the hook?"
"Headache."
"Faint smell of gas in here."
"Is there?"
Colin got up and went to the cooker, sniffed, peered and said, "The pilot light's gone out."
He relit it and asked, "A cup of tea?"
"Sit down. I'll make it."
Colin sat. Gordon filled the electric kettle, switched it on and asked, "Where's Mavis?"
"Left me."
After a moment Gordon murmured, "I see," and sat down facing him, then pointed a forefinger and said urgently, "Listen son. Listen. When a thing like this happens to a man the first thing he must do is, cut his losses."

Colin stared at him then started laughing. Three seconds later the laughter became its opposite. With elbow on table and brow on fist Colin shook with almost silent sobs. Gordon sat watching him until the kettle boiled.

18

One evening three months later Clive Evans watched a rugby match on television while Mavis lay on the hearthrug reading a Sunday paper, fingers pressing ears to shut out the commentator's gabble. The game ended. Evans switched off the set, yawned and said, "They should have won. I don't know who's to blame for the result – them, the referee or their opponents, but they should have won."

Mavis turned a page of the paper.

"I'm going out for an hour or two, Mavis. See you about eleven."

"For a drink I suppose."

"That's right."

"And I'm not coming?"

"I'll be seeing Jack and Ernie Thomson and Hamish Cunningham most likely. Do you *like* them Mavis?"

"I think they're bores."

"And you don't hide your feelings, do you? Frankly, Mavis, you're an embarrassment in certain company. Why do you want to meet my boring acquaintances?"

"I'm lonely," she said in a low voice.

Evans sighed, chose an apple from a bowl, ate it thoughtfully then said, "I'm sorry you're lonely Mavis but what can I do? We could kill the next two hours watching telly or playing rummy but that would make two people miserable instead of one. We'd be like married couples who stop each other enjoying the things they can't share so lead lives that are half envy and half boredom. I *enjoy* my boring friends. I won't stop meeting them because you don't enjoy them and have no friends of your own."

"You explain everything *beautifully*," Mavis said with a bitterness which Evans found infectious. Lifting the fruit bowl he laid it beside her saying softly, "Look Mavis! Lovely apples for you. Try one. They're delicious. And here's a bookcase half a yard away. The best minds in human history, Shakespeare, George Eliot, Agatha Christie, Edna O'Brien have sweated blood to fill these shelves for you. Or here's television, our window on the world, a choice of three windows nowadays. Not a night goes by without it showing people slaughtered by bombs in Asia or famine in Africa. Watch them doing it and feel *privileged* Mavis. Or do you want the sound of a friendly human voice? Try the telephone! Dial the speaking clock and find what the time will be on the third stroke."

His voice had grown louder but now, losing his temper, he thrust his face toward hers and said in spitting whisper, "Do anything, Mavis, but shut me up in your depressing little predicament for the next two hours."

She cried out, "I wish I hadn't sent Bill away! He loved me."

"Kids have no choice, have they?" said Evans soberly. "Funny. I never thought there was cruelty in me but when you tighten your sullen screws on me the stuff comes bubbling out, doesn't it?"

She seemed to ignore him. He put a coat on saying, "You're still a young woman. Why not try for a job?"

"What job? Nursing the sick? Wrapping biscuits in a factory?"

"Your trouble is you feel too good for the world so have to depend on people like me, who don't."

At the door he turned and said, "I still love you Mavis, as much as you let me nowadays. I'm still glad we met when you were tiring of Colin Kerr. Weeks may pass before you find a way to leave me. Let's pass them as pleasantly as possible, eh? When I come back at eleven I'll be a lot less ironical."

He left

and soon after she went to the phone and dialled. A voice said *Colin Kerr here.*

In a low voice she said, "Hullo Colin. Do you remember me?"

Mavis! How good to hear you! I was hoping you would call.

"You mean that?"

Of course.

"Would you like to see me?"

Of course. I'd have called you long ago but didn't know where you were.

"Tonight?"

Definitely.

"Could you pick me up in the car?"

No, I've sold it.

"Then I'll come by bus unless . . . Colin, is Gordon with you?"

No.
"Right, I'm leaving now. Are you sure you don't hate me?"
I love you.
"I just want to see you tonight Colin."
Fine. Do it.

19

At Saint Leonard's Bank the Colin who opened the door to her was more fleshy, more relaxed, more like his father than the Colin she remembered. He led her into a living-room where a rolled carpet lay like a felled tree trunk on bare floorboards. Windows were curtainless. All furniture but the sofa was stacked in a corner.

"You're leaving!" she said.

"That's right."

"So I've caught you on your last night in the old home?"

"O no. I'll be here till Tuesday when the furniture will be removed. Then I'll spend a week in Gordon's place, then I'll go to Zambia."

"Why?"

"To lecture in a college there."

"Why?"

"It might be more interesting. It might not, of course. Come with me and find out. But first of all, a coffee? I can also offer sherry. I still have a full bottle I bought for that disastrous party."

"Coffee please," she said smiling back at him. "I'm glad you didn't drink all the booze in the house."

He went to the kitchen. She walked to the sofa between books piled on the floor. Before she arrived he had obviously been tying his library in bundles. She sat and lit a cigarette. He returned with a loaded tray and sat beside her with the tray between them.

"Your health," he said, raising a mug of tea.

"Yours!" she said, lifting a mug of coffee. They clinked mugs and sipped.

"Life with Evans hasn't made you less beautiful Mavis."

"That's the first compliment you've ever paid to my looks, Colin Kerr! You used to take them for granted. I hated it."

He smiled back and said, "I was maybe too shy to pay compliments, but I never took your looks for granted. Have an ashtray. How's Bill?"

"He's at a boarding school."

He stared at her in horror. She said defensively, "It's a very good boarding school. His father is paying for it."

"You sent him to strangers? Maybe you're a wicked woman after all. I think, Mavis," said Colin firmly, "you had better come back to me."

"I don't recognize you, Colin."

"It's your fault . . ." (he looked down ruefully at the curve of his abdomen) ". . . whenever I feel lonely nowadays I eat. It helps."

"I'm not talking about your figure."

"I love you."

"You don't *look* unhappy."

"I'm not. I've learned to love you without that. I'm grateful, Mavis!"

"I don't know what you mean."

"Yes you do! You're responsible for it. Before we met

my life was almost wholly shaped by my father and I
didn't even know. He's such a decent man that I don't
think he knew either. Going to Cambridge changed
nothing because Cambridge was a cosy patriarchy too.
That's why I needed you who hated everything that
cramped me. So you drove Dad out and started shaping
my life yourself. Thank God you weren't a decent Scots
woman who would have kept me at my pointless job
in that dull college for the rest of my life! I've never
been good at asserting myself. But you *forced* me to
assert myself – before you cleared out."

"So now you're happy and free?" she asked sarcastically.

"I'm independent. I can be alone without going
melancholy-mad. What others think no longer worries
me much. I don't need you, Mavis, but I want you
because you're bonny and reckless and clever and
now I can love you like a man. It wasn't a man who
loved you three months ago. It was . . ." (he thought a
little then smiled with amusement and distaste) " . . .
a dog shaped like a man."

Abruptly Mavis stubbed out her cigarette and said,
"You're a stranger to me Colin."

"Good! Your life has been full of strangers. Try life
with this one."

"But you aren't the sort of stranger I like."

His smile faded. She stood up and said, "I suppose I'm
glad you're happy, Colin, but you're the sort of man I
most detest because the world is so full of you: all glib
and grinning and damnably, damnably sure of
themselves. You used to be . . . not like that. I loved you
then."

"And showed it!" he said bitterly.

With a cold little smile she said, "Goodbye Mr Kerr,"

and went too fast to the front door to be overtaken before he managed to open it for her.

"Thanks," she muttered, passing through. When she was halfway down the garden path he cried on a note of pain, "Mavis!"

She paused and looked stonily back. He said wistfully, "Good luck, Mavis!" and meant it. She suddenly smiled back with what seemed affection, shrugged her shoulders and went away. He looked after her, a hand pressing part of his stomach where twelve years later an ulcer would develop after his African wife left him.

Closing the door he returned to the living-room, lifted Mavis's quarter-smoked cigarette from the ashtray and looked at it for a long time. Then he threw it into the hearth and went on tying up his books.

FIVE

OTHER

SOBER

STORIES

A NIGHT OFF

IN 1986 THE BRITISH GOVERNMENT abolished
physical punishment in the schools it controlled. This
story is from the dark age before that happened.

1

One Friday afternoon at fifty-nine minutes and several
seconds past three o'clock a no longer young, slightly
plump teacher stood in an open doorway gazing at the
dial of his wristwatch. He concentrated on the second
hand to avoid facing a chattering queue of twelve-year-
old boys who chattered and jostled each other in ways
he despaired of preventing.

"Control yourselves, keep in line," he told them, "no
need for impatience. Every one stand still beside your
neighbour. If you aren't standing by your neighbour
when the bell rings I'll make you . . ."

An electric bell rang and the queue charged from the
room. As the boys poured past he muttered, "All right,

off you go," then closed the door behind them.

"Well McGrotty," he said striding briskly to his desk, "this is the end of the week and no doubt you're as keen to leave as I am. Let's get rid of the painful business fast. Put out your hand."

He took from the desk a leather belt which forked at the end like a snake's tongue. Raising it till the thongs fell behind his right shoulder he approached a small poorly dressed boy who stood with shoulders hunched close to ears, hands thrust deep in pockets of shorts.

"Hand out!" said the teacher again.

"Naw sir," muttered McGrotty, thrusting his hands in deeper.

"Why not?"

"I was just picknup a pencil."

The teacher sighed and said, "All right, McGrotty, since you seem in no hurry to leave we'll review your case once more. Did you hear me tell the class – the whole class – that nobody must leave their seat without first putting up their hand and asking my permission?"

"Yes sir."

"Did I also say that whoever left their seat without permission would get three of the belt?"

"Yes sir."

"And then you left your seat without permission. Yes or no?"

"Yes sir."

"So put out your hand."

"Naw sir."

"Why *not*?"

"Cos I was just picknup a pencil."

The teacher sighed again, sat at his desk and spoke
with the belt draped over his knee.

"McGrotty, I realize as well as you do that there is nothing wicked – nothing antisocial – nothing criminal in leaving a seat to pick up a dropped pencil. But we had anarchy in the classroom today. Anarchy! Pellets were fired, someone threw a book while I was getting rulers from the cupboard, whenever I turned my back somebody did something horrible to someone else. I heard you squeal loud enough. Who kicked you? You didn't have that when you came to my classroom this afternoon."

The teacher pointed to a livid bruise below McGrotty's dirty left knee cap. McGrotty glowered silently at the floor.

"Did Sludden do that?"

McGrotty said nothing.

"Did McPake?"

"I didnae do anything."

"I am perfectly aware, McGrotty, that you are neither a troublemaker nor a bully. But I cannot protect you from troublemakers and bullies in a class where nobody sits still and nobody does what I say. That is why I announced that I would give three of the belt to the first boy who left his seat without permission. Sludden and McPake knew I meant it. Why, McGrotty, why in the name of goodness didn't *you*?"

"I was just picknup a . . ."

The teacher struck a crashing blow on the desklid with the belt, sprang up and roared, "Hand out McGrotty! We've no witnesses here! If you don't take this belt on your hand you'll feel it where it lands on you!"

He advanced wielding the belt over his head. McGrotty

backed into a corner, shut his eyes tight and stuck a hand supported by the other hand as far out as possible. His face, screwed into agonized expectation of worse agony, upset the teacher who paused and pleaded, "Be a *man*, McGrotty!"

McGrotty stood still with outstretched hands and tears sliding down his cheeks. The teacher flung the belt onto his desk and sat down holding his head as if it ached. He said wearily, "Go away. Leave me alone. For God's sake leave me alone McGrotty."

Though not looking straight at the boy the teacher knew what happened next. McGrotty lowered hands, wiped cheeks with jacket sleeve, walked to the door. McGrotty opened it, stepped out, hesitated, yelled, "Ye big fat stupit wet plaster ye!" slammed the door and ran away. The teacher had no wish to run after him. His depression was not much deepened by McGrotty's parting words. He thought, "I could have belted him if I'd wanted to. He knows it and that's why he's mad at me." A minute later the teacher got up, locked the classroom cupboards, locked the classroom door behind him, followed McGrotty downstairs and gave the keys to the headmaster's secretary.

2

He was not the last teacher to leave school that Friday. At the playground gate a small three-wheeled vehicle propelled by a rear engine overtook him. This braked and the driver asked if he wanted a lift into town. He

did and climbed in beside a grey-haired woman with a
leg in a metal brace. She said, "You're usually away a
lot earlier."

"Yes, I had someone to sort out. One-B-nine got out
of hand and I had to keep the ringleader behind for
extra discipline – three of the best – wham wham
wham. I think he got the message."

"Was it Sludden?"

"No."

"McPake?"

"No."

"Who was it?"

"McGrotty."

"I've always found McGrotty a poor spiritless
creature. It's Sludden and McPake I keep my eye
on in one-B-nine."

"They never bother *me*."

"Which shows you can't generalize about children
from one class to the next. You live in town?"

"No, out Carntyne way."

"Meeting your wife in town?"

"No, Friday is my night off."

"Your night off what?"

He frowned because her terse questions made him feel
uncomfortably childish. At last he said, "Have you
noticed how almost everything we do becomes a
habit?"

"It's inevitable at our age."

"It may be inevitable but it worries me. I can stand it
at work – teaching would be impossible without
routines – but surely private life should be different?
Yet on Sunday we have the usual long lie, late breakfast

and afternoon stroll in the park. On Monday or Tuesday I change my library book, on Wednesday or Thursday a babysitter comes and we go out to a film or visit friends. And when we visit friends our conversations are much the same as last time. Never any new ideas. Never any new . . . behaviour. So on Fridays I have a night off. I go into town and let the unexpected happen."

"Does your wife take nights off?"

"She doesn't want them. Our son isn't quite two yet. But she doesn't mind me enjoying some freedom. She knows I won't get drunk, or waste money, or do anything stupid. My wife," said the teacher as if making a puzzling discovery, "is a very *intelligent* woman."

"It would seem so. Where will I drop you?"

"Anywhere near Sauchiehall Street. I'm going to the Delta tearoom."

"I can easily drop you there. Several of our staff usually meet there after school don't they? Don't Jean and Tom Forbes?"

"Yes," said the teacher defensively, "but others go there too – art students, and people who work in television and . . . journalists and . . . unconventional people like that. Interesting people."

"Then it's very wise of you to go there too."

He looked at her suspiciously. She said, "On your night off, I mean. I was an art student once. I felt wonderfully interesting in those days."

3

In the Delta tearoom three of his colleagues sat round a table in silence punctuated by occasional remarks. They had talked hard to children all day so were partly resting their voices, partly easing them back into adult conversation. As the teacher approached he heard a bearded man called Plenderleith say, "and he never starts anything."

"Mhm," said Jean, a young woman who was pleasantly vivacious most of the day but not at quarter to five on Friday afternoons. Nearby her husband Tom swiftly, steadily corrected a stack of exercise books, underlining words, scribbling marginal comments and marks out of twenty. The teacher ordered a coffee, brooded for a while then asked Plenderleith, "Who were you talking about when I came in?"

"Jack Golspie."

"Why did you say he never starts anything?"

"It's true. He waits until someone else suggests something then hangs about looking pathetic until he's included."

"Mind you it isn't easy to start something, is it? When did you last do it?"

"I don't remember. I don't care. I was just telling Jean why Jack Golspie bored me."

A waitress brought coffee. The teacher drank most of it before saying gloomily, "He bores me too."

Tom Forbes marked his last essay, put the exercise

books in a briefcase and sat back with a sigh of relief.
"It beats me how you can do that first thing after school
on Friday," said the teacher on his gloomy note. "Last
thing on Sunday evening is as soon as I can manage."

"From now onward no memory of schoolwork will
disturb the evening's joy," said Tom, yawning slightly.

"It's our wedding anniversary," Jean explained.

"Congratulations!" said the teacher, truly pleased. "The
first?"

"The first."

"Splendid. How will you celebrate?"

"A dinner for two in the Rogano first," said Tom, "then
a party."

"Definitely a party," said Jean. The teacher looked
hopefully from one to the other but they were
exchanging smiles in a way which excluded him. He
lapsed into mild depression again.

Suddenly Plenderleith muttered, "Hell."

They looked at him.

"Tony McCrimmon," he added.

"Has he seen us?" asked Jean looking down at her cup.

"No doubt of it," said Plenderleith grimly. "Here he
comes, flaunting his regalia."

The teacher saw a big black-moustached man with
close-cropped hair approach. His bulk was emphasized
by a thick overcoat with square shoulders from which
shiny camera cases hung on straps.

"Hullo hullo hullo! Still here in the customary corner?"
he said, sitting with them. "I was passing the old Delta
tearoom and thought, five o'clock on Friday! Why not
drop in and see if the old gang are in the customary

corner? So in I come and here you are."

"That's nice of you, Tony," said Jean gently.

"I think I know you. Or do I?" McCrimmon asked the teacher who found the question confusing.

"You don't," Tom told McCrimmon jovially. "You went to London months before he joined us. But he's bound to know you. Who hasn't heard the name of Tony McCrimmon?"

The teacher, embarrassed, said, "Yes, I'm sure I've heard it but I can't exactly remember where or why."

"Ahaw! Such is fame. I'm better known in Fleet Street and Soho than I'll ever be in my native land. Waitress, a coffee! Very hot, very black, very strong."

"You're a journalist?" asked the teacher, interested.

"You're getting warm, son. Yes, I wield the old plume from time to time but my forte is the pictorial genre. You may have seen something of mine in the *Sunday Times* colour supplement a wee while ago: *Britain's Forgotten Royalty*. My work."

"All of it, Tony?" Jean softly asked.

"The pictures. The idea was mine too but the writer got the credit for it. That sort of thing happens all the time. I'm used to it."

"What brings you north of Soho?" asked Plenderleith.

"Exhaustion, Plendy-boy, sheer exhaustion. I can work myself into the ground like a pig when the mood is on me but periodically I've got to stop. I throw up whatever I'm in the middle of and go somewhere quiet and . . . just let my mind go totally blank. Like the yogis. A bit of eastern mysticism is a great antidote to the commercial rat race. Willie Maugham taught me that. Ever read him?"

Again McCrimmon was looking at the teacher who replied that his field was maths and he hadn't much time for reading nowadays.

"So you're back in Glasgow for the eastern mysticism?" said Plenderleith drily.

"I know what you people think of me," McCrimmon said in a voice so quietly sincere that the three who knew him glanced uneasily at each other but relaxed when he said, "You think I'm a cynic. You think I'm a cynic because I'm dynamic and who ever heard of a dynamo with a heart? Well, *this* dynamo has a heart." (He clapped a hand to his chest.) "No matter how far I travel I'll always return to auld Scotia. A man needs roots. But," he concluded, becoming less solemn and turning to the teacher again, "you ought to read Maugham. He was a great writer but a greater human being. I got on well with him, before the end."

"You knew him?" said the teacher.

"Where's that coffee of mine?" said McCrimmon looking round. "I keep forgetting how rotten the service is here. Yes, I knew old Willie Maugham. Beaverbrook introduced us."

The photographer concentrated on the teacher with the instinct of a performer finding an audience. The quiet departure of Jean, Tom and Plenderleith was hardly noticed by the two who remained, one spouting fluent monologues, the other inciting them with exclamations and questions.

4

Four coffees later McCrimmon said, "And that is the true story of my last and worst encounter with Beaverbrook."

The teacher was excited and appalled. He had suspected great press barons were greedy, selfish and unscrupulous, but had not thought them petty, vindictive and superstitious.

"Amazing – really amazing," he murmured, "but I think the lassie wants us to leave."

The room was empty but for them and a bored waitress lounging near the till.

"Forget her – she kept me waiting for my coffee. I'm surprised that you haven't asked why I'm back in Scotland."

"You told us you were here to relax and meditate."

"Did I? So I did. I wasn't being strictly accurate. There are better places to relax than smoky old Glasgow. No laddie. I'm here with a purpose."

McCrimmon pressed his lips together and nodded heavily.

"If you'd rather not tell me –" said the teacher after a silence.

"Know something? I like you. There's not many I would waste my sweetness on but I think you're what I would call trustworthy. Notice how many new buildings are going up nowadays?"

"Yes."

"And a lot more are going to go up which means even more old stuff will be hammered down. It's inevitable. All progress is inevitable. But when these filthy old tenements and warehouses and cinemas are replaced by motorways and multistorey flats and shopping centres folk are going to miss them, hence *this* little toy –" (McCrimmon tapped a camera case with his finger) "– I paid two hundred quid down for it and it'll make my fortune. I will emerge as the Recording Angel of Glasgow's recent past."

"You won't believe this," said the teacher excitedly, "but I've thought of doing that!"

McCrimmon seemed not to believe it or found it a negligible idea in others. He said, "I'll show more than the buildings of course, I'll show the people. We don't just have smooth characterless buildings going up, we've smooth characterless people taking over. Like the three who've just left."

The teacher could not help showing surprise because he liked the three who had just left and did not think them very different from himself. McCrimmon said quickly, "Don't get me wrong – they're nice enough folk but speaking as an artist you cannae beat the hard dour folk formed by the First World War, the General Strike, the Thirties' Depression and the single-room flat – the faces of folk who took abject poverty for granted. Closet-on-the-stair faces. Jawbox-with-one-brass-swan-neck-cold-water-tap faces. Black-leaded-kitchen-range-with-polished-steel-trim faces. There aren't many left."

"A lot of folk still live like that," said the teacher with a faint smile.

"I wish I knew where. All the single-end flats I've seen this week had a tiled fireplace and modern sink unit with gas water-heater. What's wrong with you?" he asked, for the teacher, gripped by a strong idea,

stared at him like an equal and said, "Are you free just
now Tony? Because if you are I can take you to exactly
the place you want – recess bed, jawbox, polished fire
range, wally dugs, the lot."
"Who does it belong to?"
"My granny and grampa – my father's folk."
"What sort of faces have they?"
"Good faces. Kind faces. Lots of character in them."
"Wrinkles?"
"They're in their eighties. They live overby in the Cow-
caddens. I'd love a record of them. I'd pay you for it."
McCrimmon stood up and slung his cases round him
saying, "I suppose they may have some sociological
value. Let's go."

McCrimmon held aloof while the teacher paid for
the coffees but walked beside him up Sauchiehall Street
and over Rose Street in the dusk of an autumn evening.
The teacher explained he must first buy some presents
as he had not visited his grandparents for over a year.
"Coloured beads to keep the natives happy, eh?" said
McCrimmon. The teacher did not answer. He supposed
that McCrimmon's talent had destroyed normal
sympathies by raising him into a bad-mannered class
which must be tolerated because it knows no better.

5

They crossed New City Road into a district which two
years before had been lively with people and bright
with small shops. An advancing motorway now

threatened it with demolition so nothing was being replaced or repaired and people with plans for the future had moved out. Pavements were cracked, road surfaces potholed, some tenements obviously derelict. Not every shop was boarded up. In a small general store the teacher bought bread, butter, jam, cheese, eggs, potatoes, tinned corned beef, sardines, beans and stewed pears. The Pakistani owner put all this in a cardboard box which the teacher hoisted upon his shoulder.

He led McCrimmon into a gaslit close and up narrow stairs with the door of a communal lavatory on each half landing. On the third landing he tapped a door with signs of former working-class dignity: a shiningly polished brass door-knob, letter-box and name-plate engraved with the name ROSS.

"Who's there?" asked an old voice from within.

"It's me, Granny – Jimmy."

"O my boy!"

A small neat timidly smiling woman opened the door. She wore spectacles, flower-patterned wrap-round apron and old cloth slippers. She looked much older than the teacher remembered. One reason why he visited her so seldom was that she looked older every time he did so. He said, "I've brought a friend, Granny."

"I'm sure he's welcome."

"Hullo hullo Mrs Ross. McCrimmon is the name but you just call me Tony."

"Fancy that. Come in Mr McCrimmon."

They entered a small neat room with a recess bed in which the teacher's father's father lay perfectly still on his back. A wedge of pillows propped him at a straight angle from waist to head. His eyes were shut, mouth slightly open, spectacles pushed onto brow, hands folded on book on coverlet over stomach.

"How's Grampa?" the teacher murmured placing the box on a sideboard.

"O don't ask me," she sighed, "I've given up worrying about him. Just be a bit quiet and we'll have a sip of tea without being bothered by his nonsense. Or do you want me to make you a meal?" she asked, staring at the groceries.

"No Granny, I'm afraid we can't stay long. A cup of tea will do."

"You're a good wee boy to play Santa Claus with your old folk."

At the side of the range was a kettle of water which she shifted onto the fire saying, "Take off your coat and sit down Mr McCrimmon."

Her grandson had already done so.

"Don't worry about me Mrs Ross," said McCrimmon strolling to the wooden sink before the window. He stood there with his back to the room. The teacher felt dominated by his grandfather's lean, Caesar-like profile and whispered, "Is his back still bad?"

"Yes but he never speaks about it now."

"Can't you get a doctor to him?"

"You know what he thinks about doctors. Come to the fire, Mr McCrimmon. Make yourself at home."

"Just don't worry about me Mrs Ross," said McCrimmon without turning round.

The kettle simmered. Mrs Ross brewed a pot of tea

asking, "How's the family?"

"Not bad. All right. You should visit us. You'd like the wee boy."

"It's difficult getting away from here without a babysitter."

She nodded to the bed.

"Aye. She means me," said his grandfather opening his eyes. "She needna. I can manage without her."

His distinct low-keyed voice seemed to fill the room. His wife gave an incredulous "Hm!" and laid on the table a plate of biscuits and tea things. Mr Ross adjusted his spectacles with careful arm movements which left the trunk of his body perfectly still, and appeared to resume reading his library book. Mrs Ross poured tea into a mug and three cups. To the mug she added sugar, milk, a long straw, then placed it by the bed on a cabinet holding a chamberpot. The teacher and his grandmother sat at the table drinking tea as McCrimmon, ignoring another invitation to join them, examined something in his hand.

Abruptly Mr Ross said, "How's the teaching going?"

"On," said the teacher. "And on. And on."

"Aye! It's secure."

"Secure, yes. Only a sex crime will get me out of it now."

"And well paid, compared with what most manual workers earn. And worthwhile. Children's minds need feeding as much as their bodies. A conscientious teacher has every right to respect himself."

"I would if I was any good at it."

"If you are bad at it only two explanations are possible:

you have not yet learned how to do it properly or you are teaching the wrong thing. What is your pal playing at?"

"This is a light meter Mr Ross," said McCrimmon watching the instrument in his hand. The teacher said hurriedly, "Tony's a famous photographer Grampa –"

"Does he meter light from force of habit?"

"Your grandson invited me because I am making a pictorial social survey, Mr Ross, a record of the life of Glasgow. And by life I mean more than the shape of the buildings. I want the world to know how decent, hardworking people live in Glasgow Anno Domini nineteen sixty-five. I doubt I'll ever find a more decent working-class home than this."

"You cannae photograph in here Mr McCrimmon!" cried Mrs Ross. "The place is like a midden and I'm no dressed right."

"Your place is as neat as a new pin Mrs Ross and so are you."

"I havenae dusted since this morning!"

"I see no dust and what I don't see my camera won't show."

"Don't let him do it, John!" the woman begged her husband who said as if to himself, "A pictorial social survey. What good will it do?"

"Have you heard of Matthew Brady, Mr Ross?"

"No."

"Have you heard of the Depression and the American dust bowl and the New Deal?"

"Aye."

"Well, President Roosevelt was persuaded to set up the New Deal by Matthew Brady's photographs of how decent honest American working-class families had to live in the American dust bowl. Now, I don't claim to be another Matthew Brady, but I believe that a photographer without a social conscience is an enemy of the human race. You know as well as I do that thousands of working people – some of them bedridden like you – live in single rooms with an outside lavatory they cannae reach because of the stairs. Not everyone in Britain knows that. Some very well-off folk prefer not to know it. Harold Wilson says he's going to improve the quality of British life but has anyone shown him what life is like in Glasgow? Harold Macmillan said the British worker has never had it so good. But is it good *enough*?"

After a pause Mr Ross said firmly, "It is NOT good enough."

"Then you'll let me try to do something about it?"

After a pause Mr Ross picked up his book, appeared to read it again and muttered, "Go ahead."

Swiftly McCrimmon unpacked his camera, clipped on a flash mechanism and snapped the still figure in the bed from several angles. Then he said, "You next Mrs Ross."

"No. On no," she said firmly, "I'm not going to have a lot of total strangers staring at me. It wouldnae be right."

"You never told me to expect anything like this," muttered McCrimmon, scowling at the teacher. Ten minutes passed before Mrs Ross was persuaded to sit. "Don't let them make me do it, John," she begged her husband. He said, "You might as well, Beth. The pictures

won't appear in any papers sold in this area. If they're
printed in a book Glasgow libraries won't stock it. Snap
her quick, McCrimmon."

"Hector's photographed the queen, Granny!" said
the teacher. "You're as important as the queen is. If
the queen gets photographed by Tony McCrimmon
why shouldn't you?"

At last she consented to sit in her rocking-chair with
the tea things beside her, both hands thrust out of sight
in her apron pocket and the kettle on the range blowing
a faint cloud of steam behind. She gasped each time
the flash exploded but kept the unyielding expression
of a martyred stoic.

"Your tea will be cold now," said Mr Ross, shakily
putting down the mug with the straw which he had
sucked a little. "Drink it up Mr McCrimmon and she'll
make another pot while you tell me more about this
Matthew Brady and his impact on the American dust
bowl."

"No tea for me," said McCrimmon swiftly packing,
"I'm already late for my next appointment. But my
time has not been wasted. You have both added to
the fruitfulness of what promises to have been a
rewarding evening . . . Coming?" he asked the
teacher.

"I'm afraid I must go, Granny. Tony and me have
this appointment. But I'll be back soon, probably with
Lorna and the boy. Good night Grandad."

"Aye," said Mr Ross.

As Mrs Ross helped the teacher on with his coat
she murmured, "Yes, bring Lorna and the laddie soon

– but don't bring *him*."

"I won't."

"Will we be paid anything for all that fuss?"

"I don't know Granny."

"A bit of extra money would be a help now he never leaves his bed."

"I'm not rushing you! Stay here if you like," called McCrimmon from the landing. The teacher followed McCrimmon downstairs. Though admiring how the photographer had managed his grandfather the visit had not left him happier. He also wished he had not suggested he would soon return with his wife and child. That would never happen. Lorna hated slums and the Cowcaddens had become one. At the close mouth McCrimmon said, "A very punishing session. For God's sake lead me to a pub."

6

Two hours later they sat in a noisy overcrowded lounge bar, the teacher brooding over the visit to his grandparents and trouble with McGrotty. He wondered why they worried him equally. The money he was spending on drink for McCrimmon also worried him. The photographer kept ordering pints of Guinness with large malt whiskies. This sacrifice to Bohemian good-fellowship had brought the teacher no greater liveliness, no brighter sense of social existence. He felt feeble and dull and oppressed by loud voices from adjacent conversations.

"So this big blonde with the huge tits walks straight

up to me and says, 'Is there anything you would like sir?' HAW HAW HAW."

"Thistle is a rotten team. The Thistle hasnae a chance. Our lot will walk over them. Our lot will walk right over them and trample them into the ground."

"And that is the true story of my last and worst encounter with Beaverbrook, but I confess to pangs of injured vanity laddie. I seem to be casting pearls of wisdom into unreceptive ears."

A barmaid placed a Guinness and a Macallan before McCrimmon. The teacher reached into his pocket saying gloomily, "I'll pay."

"You'll have to, laddie. The McCrimmon wallet is not in the best of health."

There was silence between them for many minutes.

"Queer about that old woman," said McCrimmon suddenly.

"What old woman?"

"That old-age-pensioner. Your granny. Did you notice her primitive reaction to this?" (McCrimmon touched his camera.) "She definitely did not want to be photographed."

"She was shy. A lot of people hate being stared at by strangers."

"What is shyness? Irrational terror. Your granny is like African blacks who think anyone who takes their picture has captured their souls. And we find the same superstition in the wife of a Glaswegian industrial serf! We have not advanced as far above the ape as our atom-splitting technology suggests."

"You annoy me sometimes."

"Tell me more, laddie."

"You keep changing your story. You told me you wanted a record of folk in the old tenements because there was something fine and artistic about them. You told my grandad . . ."

"I know what I told your grandad. Did I contradict myself? Very well, I contradicted myself. I am vast. I contain multitudes. Don't try to shut Tony McCrimmon into your toty-wee mental filing cabinet, laddie. He won't fit. He's too big."

With an appearance of great satisfaction McCrimmon swallowed his Macallan. The teacher, crushed by the toper's superior intellect, heard a bell ring and the bar manager shout, "Last orders ladies and gentlemen. Your last chance of a drink before closing time."

"What *use* is life Tony?" asked the teacher desperately. "Is there a purpose in it, a way to make it better, or should we just suffer and survive? I'm asking you because I know you won't give a religious answer. I don't like religion. My mother was a Catholic who had to leave the church because she married a Protestant. She died thinking she would go to hell because of that. I *know* she didn't go to hell. I *know* there's no afterlife so I can't be religious. But I want to believe *something*."

"Quite right, religion's just pie in the sky, OVER HERE DEARIE!" roared McCrimmon waving imperiously to the barmaid. "Purpose of life et cetera? In two words? Get me the same again and I will give you . . . the entire scenario and destination of our existence . . . in a coupla words."

The teacher bought the same again and waited while McCrimmon, frowning deeply, refreshed himself with thoughtful swallows.

"Feel good," he announced abruptly. "Feel good is what the life-force in each one of us decrees. Hemingway said it. Agree with him."
"I can't!" cried the teacher, exasperated. "I only feel good by accident. Nothing I plan to do or try to do makes *me* feel good and the harder I try the worse I feel. But what I most hate is that nobody respects me. Why should they? What is there in me to respect? Yet look at my grandad and granny. They've had rotten lives compared with mine, overworked and underpaid when not downright unemployed. Their most prosperous times were during two world wars. They never expected to feel good but they're still better people than me. They have dignity. I think my grandad will be dead in a year or less, and knows it, but is dying with dignity because he respects himself. I think my granny knows it too and is helping him, though God knows what will become of her when she's left with nobody. No wonder I hate visiting them. They make me ashamed of myself."
"I can explain all that," said McCrimmon with a slight hiccup. "You see there are always two main types in this world of ours, always have been, always will be: aristocrats and serfs. The aristocrats are the feel-goods – the five per cent born into the dolce vita. Eating, drinking, clothing, housing, fucking is no problem to that class because they have everything money can buy. Their only work is issuing orders and pulling off money deals. They enjoy that because it proves how important they are. The other class are the serfs whose only

satisfaction in life – if they can get it – is doing a job that thousands of others would do just as well if they dropped down dead. Religion was once the opium of the serfs but nowadays it's socialism. Is your grandad a socialist?"

"Yes – Independent Labour Party. He knew Jimmy Maxton."

"I thought so. An industrial serf who wants to abolish the aristocracy. He probably thought Utopia was dawning after the war when Attlee nationalized the mines and transport and health services."

"What about me?" cried the teacher. "What about you, for that matter?"

"We are the God-damned bourgeoisie – the middle or muddle class, son. The aristos, you see, don't know how to talk to serfs because they speak a different language. So they pay folk from serf backgrounds a bit extra to help them manage the rest. So we get foremen and sergeant majors and policemen and lawyers and civil servants and teachers like you. And since aristos hate entertaining each other with anything but sex they pay big money to folk who can manufacture the dolce vita for them: chefs and clothes designers and models and prostitutes and artists and talented photographers like me. You need talent to enjoy the dolce vita if you arenae an aristocrat. For the rest it isnae so easy."

"Does all that . . . waffle . . . mean I cannae enjoy myself because I've no special talent?"

"If the cap fits wear it, son. And if you're one of the majority who would rather not face facts then all I can advise is *nil desperandum* and soldier on with the fixed grin of an idiot."

The teacher shook his head hopelessly. McCrimmon's speech reminded him of a Marxist uncle whose speeches had bored him when he was small, yet McCrimmon was certainly no Marxist.

Then he heard the bell ring again and the bar manager shout, "Time up ladies and gentlemen! Drink up and clear out! You've had your fun so hurry along! Some of us have beds to go to!"

"Christ," groaned McCrimmon between swigs of porter, "why am I in a city . . . largest in a so-called *country* . . . where pubs shut at half past nine? Scotland is afflicted by three plagues. The first . . . ignorance of life. Third . . . envy of success. Second is . . . God it's hot in here. What did I say third was?"

"Envy of success."

"I was right. Let's clear out. Where," McCrimmon demanded on the pavement outside, "where can we go? Where's the party? There's always a party somewhere."

The teacher had drunk very little compared with McCrimmon. The cool night air restored his mental clarity. He knew that the comfort of home was the best he would get but longing for one sip of unfamiliar social pleasure made him linger and murmur that Tom and Jean Forbes were having a party to celebrate their first wedding anniversary – they had told him so without inviting him to it; he might not be welcome.

"Forget Tom and Jean Forbes," cried McCrimmon, putting an arm round the teacher's shoulder and marching him westward, "I'll be your entrance ticket, son. Nobody can shut out The Vivid Scotchman. That's what they call me in Soho – The Vivid Scotchman. Over breakfast this morning I promised myself a wank or a woman before another day dawned. With a party looming up the latter option becomes a practical certainty."

7

The Forbes lived in the top flat of a spacious nineteenth-century tenement. Tom opened the front door and said pleasantly, "Hullo! So you both found your way here after all."

"Time has not blunted your acute powers of observation Tommy," said McCrimmon strolling in with the teacher behind him.

"Drop you coats in there," said Tom pointing to a bedroom. "If you're hungry there's plenty to eat in the kitchen but I'm afraid the booze is running out."

"I've heard that one before," said McCrimmon grimly. A slender girl in jeans, checked blouse and open sheepskin coat stood within the bedroom door. McCrimmon paused and said to her on a note of gentle astonishment, "Hullo, long time no see. How are you getting on? Someone told me you were engaged. Who's the lucky fellow?"

"I'm not engaged and I'm getting on quite well."

"You don't remember me?"

"I don't. I'm sorry," said the girl. The teacher dropped his coat on a pile of coats on the bed, regretting his connection with McCrimmon. He was embarrassed by hearing him say, "Don't apologize, I feel the same way. As soon as I saw your face I realized I'd known it for years though I've never met you before in my life. That gives us something to celebrate, eh? Let's find where they've hidden the booze. I think you can help me with a couple of *Sunday Times* articles I'm taking pictures for."

"I can't, I'm waiting for a friend."

"Bring her too. Bring him if he's a boyfriend. Romance, not sex is what I'm after. Romance and glamour are the raw materials of my profession. Sex is a distraction. You are perfectly safe with me."

The teacher hurried into the lobby.

Only a husband and wife who both earned professional wages could afford such a flat, thought the teacher enviously. The ceilings were over twice the height of those in his semi-detached council house. He peeped into a living-room which could have held his own living-room and the kitchen beside it and the two bedrooms and bathroom above. Politely chatting well-dressed people showed this was not a suddenly improvised party but one whose guests had been invited days, perhaps weeks before. The crippled teacher who had given him a lift sat by the fire talking with Jean so he recoiled into the lobby. *Friday night is my night off*, he had told her, *I go into town and let the unexpected happen*. If she saw him she would know he had gatecrashed. At the end of a short corridor he found a kitchen where chatting couples and trios were so tightly packed that a lonely man was not noticeable.

Filling a plate with salad and cold meat he stood eating with a fork in a corner by a refrigerator. Again voices pressed painfully in on him.

"It's a good wee car. It's not a great wee car but it's not a bad wee car. Anyway it suits me."

"Take it easy. Let yourself go. What use is worrying? That's my philosophy."

"I said you've stopped trying. You've let yourself go. You're sliding to the bottom I told him, but you aren't going to take me with you."

These did not shut out earlier voices.

"You need talent to enjoy the dolce vita."

"He never starts anything. He waits until someone else suggests something then hangs about hoping to be included."

"Ye big fat stupit wet plaster ye!"

"I could have belted him if I'd wanted to," thought the teacher unhappily then a sound recalled him wholly to the present. Through a lull in surrounding talk came the pure voice of a singer: *"I never will marry, I'll be no man's wife, I have vowed to be single, All the days of my life."*
He set down the plate and went toward the music.

In a dim room next door a dozen people sat or squatted on the carpet listening to a plain stout woman of forty or fifty who sat on a sofa under a standard lamp. With hands folded on lap she sang of hopeless love, sudden death and failed endeavour, sang so sweetly, quietly and firmly that the teacher felt her singing was the one truly good thing he had met that day and for many days. He was grateful. He was even grateful to Plenderleith who sat by the singer striking quiet harmonious chords on a guitar. She sang *Barbara Allan, The Bonnie Earl of Murray, Henry Martin* then coughed, blew out her cheeks and said, "That's all tonight folks."

The audience did not move. A girl begged, "One more?"

"Right, a short one. *Bonnie George Campbell* . . . Don't try to accompany this," she told Plenderleith and sang,

> *"High in the Highlands and low upon Tay,*
> *Bonnie George Campbell rode out on a day,*
> *Saddled and bridled and gallant rade he,*
> *Hame cam his guid horse, but never cam he."*

During the last verse the teacher was gripped by an audacious notion which made him tremble with excitement.

> *"Doon cam his auld mither greetin' fu sair,*
> *Doon cam his bonny bride rivin' her hair –*
> *'My meadow's unreaped and uncut is my corn,*
> *My barn is unfilled and my babe is unborn.'* Now

give me something to drink because my belly thinks my throat's cut," said the singer. There was a murmur of laughter and applause and someone handed her a glass of wine. The teacher hurried over to Plenderleith and said urgently, "Do you remember *On Duty*, Plendy?"

"Eh?"

"*On Duty – A Tale of the Crimea*. I sang it on the staff outing to Largs."

"Yes?"

"I'm going to sing it now. Vamp along with me will you? It's an easy tune – *dee dum dum dum dumpty, dee dum dum dum dum* – you can do it."

Plenderleith looked thoughtfully at the teacher for a

moment then shrugged and said, "All right."

"LADIES AND GENTLEMEN!" cried the teacher loudly, "ladies and gentlemen I don't know who the last singer was but we must all agree she was splendid! Wonderful! Sublime! But she sang nothing very patriotic, did she? So it is now both my duty and my pleasure to give you a rendition of that popular patriotic ballad, *On Duty – A Tale of the Crimea*. Would someone near the door switch on the ceiling light? This ballad goes better without moody lighting. Thank you! Here it comes – *On Duty – A Tale of the Crimea*."

Standing to attention like a soldier on parade he sang,

"The place was the Crimea, the year fifty-four,
When passions had unleashed the demon of war . . ."

Most of the audience were rising to leave when he made his announcement but paused to hear the start of the song. It glorified the charge of the Light Brigade, in such melodramatic clichés that the teacher's Marxist uncle had amused family gatherings by singing it with an appearance of solemnity. Nobody here seemed to understand the joke, no matter how rigidly the teacher stood and how loudly he sang in the dialect of an English officer, so he changed to a London cockney dialect. Halfway through the second verse his only audience was an old smiling man in an easy chair and the former singer. When the teacher faltered into silence the old man said, "Go on! You're doing fine!"

Nursing the glass of wine on her lap the singer said kindly, "Don't worry son, it happens to all of us sometimes. It's happened to me."

"Sorry. I'm sorry," said the teacher, "I'm very sorry."
He went to a sideboard and stood with hands in pockets staring at a framed print of van Gogh sunflowers. He would have liked to flee through the lobby and out of the house but dreaded coming face to face with another human being. Noticing Plenderleith beside him he muttered, "Sorry about that. I'm no use, you know."

"Have a nut," said Plenderleith offering a dish of salted peanuts. The teacher took and nibbled some.

"What are you no use at?" asked Plenderleith. The teacher brooded on this, sighed and said, "I envy Tony McCrimmon."

"Why?"

"He enjoys life. He appreciates himself."

"I doubt it."

"Why?"

"He talks too loud."

"I know what you mean. Yes, he blusters and bullies and ignores people's feelings but, well, I think he's entitled to do that. He's made something of himself. He's a talented photographer."

"He's a rotten photographer."

"But he works for the *Sunday Times*!"

"A year ago they used one or two of his photographs, that's all," said Plenderleith between crunching on peanuts. "When he first landed in London he bluffed his way into one or two worthwhile commissions – they were never renewed. People soon saw through him. Of course he drinks like a fish, which doesn't help. Have another nut."

The teacher stared at him blankly then nodded and hurried from the room.

He found McCrimmon in the crowded living-room talking to a blonde girl in a very short black dress and fish-net stockings. He had backed her into a corner and was saying in exasperated tones, "I am not asking you to do it nude. You wouldn't need to wear less than, shall we say, the briefest of brief bikinis!"

"I'm not interested!" said the girl. "Get it into your head that I don't want to talk about it, let alone do it!"

"Tony," said the teacher.

"But there's *money* in it," cried McCrimmon, "big money! You're the type they go for . . ."

"Excuse us Tony," said Jean walking round him and placing an arm on the girl's shoulder. "Rita, there's somebody over here who wants a private word with you. Sorry Tony."

She led the girl away.

"My God," said McCrimmon turning and surveying the room with disgust, "what a party. Cheap food, no booze and the most frigid women I've met in my life."

"Tony," said the teacher.

"What do you want?"

"I want to buy that film from you."

"What film?"

"The film in that camera —" (McCrimmon still wore his overcoat with the gear of his profession hung from the shoulders) "— the film with the photos of my granny and grampa in it."

"You do not understand photography, son. *I* own the copyright of everything I take. In the course of time I will send you a sheet of contact prints from which you may select those you would like which I will then enlarge. But remember this, it won't be cheap."

"That's not what I asked you to do. I said I would pay you to photograph my granny and grampa. You did it and now I want the film."

"I don't get this!" said McCrimmon shaking his head. "You make me photograph your old folk – make them sit for me – then without a word of explanation you ask for the undeveloped film!"

"No. I'm *telling* you to sell me the undeveloped film. Here and now! At once!"

McCrimmon turned his back and shouldered his way into the lobby saying, "Sorry son, you cannae afford it."

"Hand that film over Tony," cried the teacher, following.

"I get it! You're jealous!" said McCrimmon facing him again. "You're jealous like all the others. You cannae see someone do something original and artistic without wanting to throw your own miserable wee brick at it. Your trouble, Jimmy, is your totally third-rate mind . . ."

"You're a liar McCrimmon," said the teacher feeling his face get hot and speaking with a voice which grew suddenly huge, "a liar, a bully, a boaster, a phony and a failure! What could be more third-rate than you? – You drunken idiot!"

He glared at McCrimmon and in the silence which followed knew many were watching him and that he had never spoken so nastily to a human being before, not even to the worst of his pupils. His muscles were tensed for a fight but McCrimmon replied with unexpected dignity.

"You're wrong. I may be a failure and drunkard and

. . . and other things but I am not third-rate. Second-rate yes, all right, but not third-rate. At least I've tried to get out of the rut. I failed, true. You havenae even tried."

"The film Tony," said the teacher implacably. "Give it me."

"No."·

McCrimmon moved away. The teacher seized and jerked the strap of the camera case. It broke. With the case swinging from the strap in one hand the teacher hurried down the lobby fumbling for the lid with the other. Roaring horribly McCrimmon leapt after him and grabbed him low from behind in a rugby tackle. The camera slid out of the case and hit the floor with a sharp crack as the teacher fell face down behind it with McCrimmon on top. There was a hubbub of voices. The weight on the teacher's back was removed. Kneeling up he saw McCrimmon also kneeling, held back by men grasping each arm. Without lifting the camera the teacher opened it, pulled out the film, exposed it, dropped it and stood up, breathing heavily. Everyone looked at McCrimmon. He seemed so horrified that his captors, feeling him harmless, let him go. He crawled to the camera and lifted it with something like the unbelief of a mother lifting a dead baby. In a faint female falsetto he crooned, "Broke. My camera. Oh and it wasnae insured, it wasnae insured." He wept.

The teacher found Tom Forbes beside him saying, "Here's your coat."

"Thanks."

They went to the front door. Tom opened it. The teacher paused a moment and slid his arms into the sleeves saying, "I'm sorry about all this . . ."

"Just go home to your wife, Jimmy. Good night."

"Good night. See you on Monday . . ."

The door closed behind him.

8

The time was eighteen minutes past midnight. At one a.m. buses left Glasgow's central square for the suburbs but rather than wait for one the teacher walked five or six miles along Sauchiehall Street, Parliamentary Road and Alexandra Parade: thoroughfares of shops and tenements which in twenty years would be reshaped, shrunk or abolished by pedestrianization and a motorway system. But the teacher was thinking of the recent past. Since his last class became unruly that afternoon it had all been disastrous. The only action he did not regret was the exposure of McCrimmon's film.

"No more nights off for me," he thought. "No more nights off for me."

He also resolved to visit his grandparents again tomorrow, or on Sunday, or perhaps the following weekend. There came a fall of rain so slight that he hardly noticed it until he saw privet hedges round the Carntyne gardens glittering under the street lamps. He may not have felt exactly like Ulysses landing on the coast of Ithaca but while turning the key of his front door and quietly entering years seemed to have passed since he left for work that morning.

In the living-room his wife, who disliked going to bed alone, lay dozing on a sofa before the fire. Opening her eyes she smiled and said, "Hullo."

He tried to smile back. She said, "Bad?"

"Bad."

"Worse than last week?"

"Aye."

"What went wrong?"

"The whole day went wrong. I'll tell you tomorrow. How's the lad?"

"Not a cheep from him."

"Next week," said the teacher watching himself in a mirror above the mantelpiece, "I'll be thirty-four."

"You poor pathetic middle-aged soul," said his wife standing up and laughing and leaning on his shoulder. "Has that been worrying you?"

"A bit. Let's have a keek at him."

They went quietly upstairs to a bedroom holding a child's cot and switched on a low light in one corner. The cot contained a not quite two-year-old child soundly sleeping. His snub-nosed head with mouth pouting like a bird's blunt beak was larger than a baby's head but still babyish. On the coverlet lay a plastic duck, his mother's hairbrush and a small red motor car. The teacher bent to kiss him but was restrained by his wife's hand. She switched the light out and they tiptoed to the room next door.

Sitting on the bed he unlaced and removed his shoes saying in a baffled voice, "You . . . and that wee boy in there . . . are the only worthwhile things I know."

"What's wrong with that?"

"A man should have something more in life than his family. I used to think it would be my work but it isn't my work. I don't know what it is."

"I'll help you look for it tomorrow," said his wife gently rumpling his hair.

"No use, I'll never find it now," he said, smiling at her in a way which showed he felt much better.

"Perhaps wee Jimmy will find it."

"O yes," he said yawning, "put it off for another generation."

"You need your bed my lad," she said.

They went to bed.

MISTER
GOODCHILD

"NOBODY OVER FIFTY can tell where or how they'll live a few months hence Mrs . . . Mrs?"

"Dewhurst."

"Look at me, for instance. A year ago I was headmaster of a very good comprehensive school in Huddersfield. My wife made me take early retirement for the good of *her* health – not mine. She thought the warmer climate in the south would suit her so down to Berkshire we came. Fat lot of good *that* did. A fortnight after settling into the new house she died of a stroke. Since I do not intend to follow her example I will pause here for a few seconds Mrs . . . Mrs?"

"Dewhurst. Let me carry that," she said, pausing at a bend in the staircase.

"No no!" he said putting a cumbersome suitcase down on a higher step without releasing the handle. "I was talking about losing my wife. Well my son has a garage with five men working under him in Bracknell. 'Come and live with us, Dad,' says he, 'we've tons of room.' Yes, they have. New house with half an acre of garden.

Huge open-plan living-room with dining alcove. *Five*
bedrooms no less, one for marital couple, one each for my two grandchildren, one for guests and one for poor old grandad. But poor old grandad's bedroom is on the small side, hardly bigger than a cupboard and although I have retired from education I have not retired from public life. I am now ready to proceed – to *continue* proceeding – upward Mrs . . . Dewhurst."
They continued proceeding upward.
"I edit the You See Monthly Bulletin, the newsletter of the Urban Conservation Fellowship and that requires both space and privacy. 'Use the living-room!' says my son, 'it's big enough. The kids are at school all day and if you work at the sun patio end Myra won't disturb you.' Myra did. How could I get a steady day's work done in a house where lunch arrived any time between twelve and one? I didn't complain but when I asked for a shelf in the fridge where I could keep my own food to make my own lunch she took it for a slight on her housekeeping. So *this*!" said Mr Goodchild putting the suitcase down, "is my fourth home since last September. I'm glad my things arrived."

He stood beside Mrs Dewhurst in a high-ceilinged room that had been the master bedroom eighty years earlier when the mansion housed a family and six servants. An ostentatiously solid bed, wardrobe, dressing-table and set of chairs survived from that time. The gas heater in the hearth of a white marble fireplace was recent, also a Formica-topped table, Laura Ashley window curtains, wall-to-wall fitted carpet with jagged green and black pattern. The carpet was mostly covered by twenty-three full cardboard boxes, a heap of metal struts and shelving, a heavy old typewriter, heavier Grundig tape player, a massive black slide and picture projector called an epidiascope which looked as clumsy as its name.

"I am monarch of all I survey, my right there is none to dispute," said Mr Goodchild. "Forgive me for stating the obvious Mrs Dewhurst, but you are NOT the pleasant young man who showed me this room two days ago and asked for – and received! – what struck me as an unnecessarily huge advance on the rent."

He smiled at her to show this was a question. Without smiling back she told him the young man was an employee of the letting agency and she did not know his name because that sort come and go; she, however, lived in the basement with her husband who cleaned the hall and stairs and shared bathroom. He also looked after the garden. It was her job to collect the rent, change sheets, pillowcases and towels once a fortnight and also handle complaints.

"You will hear no complaints from me or about me, Mrs Dewhurst. A quiet, sensible, sober man I am, not given to throwing wild parties but tolerant of neighbours who may be younger and less settled. Who, exactly, are my neighbours on this floor?"

"A couple of young women share the room next door. They do something secretarial in the office of the biscuit factory."

"Boyfriends?"

"I haven't bothered to ask, Mr Goodchild."

"Admirable! Who's above and who's below?"

"The Wilsons are above and the Jhas are below: both

married couples."

"My age or yours Mrs Dewhurst? For I take you to be a youthful thirty-five or so."

A very slight softening in Mrs Dewhurst's manner confirmed Mr Goodchild's guess that she was nearly his own age. She told him that the Wilsons were young doctors and would soon be leaving for a bigger place because Mrs Wilson was pregnant; that Mr Jha had a grocery in a poorer part of town, his wife was much younger than him with a baby, a very quiet little thing, Mr Goodchild would hardly notice it.

"Jha," said Mr Goodchild thoughtfully. "Indian? Pakistani? African? *West* Indian?"

"I don't know, Mr Goodchild."

"Since I have no prejudice against any people or creed on God's earth their origin is immaterial. And now I will erect my possessions into some kind of order. Cheerio and off you go Mrs Dewhurst."

Off she went and Mr Goodchild's air of mischievous good humour became one of gloomy determination.

He hung his coat and jacket in the wardrobe. He unpacked from his suitcase a clock and radio which he put on the mantelpiece, underwear he laid in dressing-table drawers, pyjamas he placed under the pillow of the bed. Carrying the still heavy suitcase into a kitchenette he took out bottles, packets, tins and placed them in a refrigerator and on shelves. This tiny windowless space had once been the master's dressing-room and had two doors, one locked with a putty-filled keyhole. This useless door had once opened into the bedroom of the mistress, a room now rented by the secretaries. Mr Goodchild laid an ear to it, heard nothing and sighed. He had never lived alone before and sounds of occupancy would have soothed him.

In the main room he rolled up shirtsleeves, produced a Swiss army knife, opened the screwdriver attachment and by twenty minutes to six had efficiently erected four standing shelf units. Returning to the kitchenette he washed hands and put a chop under the grill. Faint voices from the next room showed it was occupied though the tone suggested a television play. He opened tins of soup, peas and baby potatoes and heated them in saucepans which he clattered slightly to let the secretaries know they too were no longer alone. Ten minutes later he ate a three-course dinner: first course, soup; second, meat with two vegetables; third, cold apple tart followed by three cups of tea. Meanwhile he listened to the six o'clock news on the BBC Home Service. Having washed, dried and put away the kitchenware he brooded long and hard over the positions of the rented furniture.

The Formica-topped table would be his main work surface so had better stand against the wall where the wardrobe now was with his shelf units on each side of it. He would shift the small bedside table to the hearthrug and dine on that. The dressing-table would go beside the bed and support the bedside lamp and his bedtime cup of cocoa. The wardrobe could then stand where the dressing-table had been. The boxes on the floor would make these shifts difficult so he piled as many as possible onto and under the bed. The hardest task was moving the wardrobe. It was eight feet high, four wide and a yard deep. Mr Goodchild, though less than average height, was proud of his ability to make heavy furniture walk across a room by pivoting it on alternate corners. The top part of the wardrobe rested on a base with a deep drawer inside. He discovered these were separate when, pivoting the base, the top section began sliding off. He dropped the base with a floor-shuddering thump. The upper part teetered with a jangling of wire coathangers but did not topple. Mr Goodchild sat down to recover from the shock. There came a tap upon the door and a voice with a not quite English accent said, "Are you all right in there?"

"Yes yes. Yes yes."

"That was one heck of a wallop."

"Yes I'm . . . shifting things about a bit Mr . . . Jha?"

"Yes?"

"I've just moved in and I'm shifting things about. I'll be at it for another hour or two."

"Exercise care please."

Mr Goodchild returned to the wardrobe and wrestled with it more carefully.

Two hours and several heavy thumps later the furniture was where he wanted it and he unpacked his possessions, starting with a collection of taped music. After putting it on a shelf beside the Grundig he played Beethoven symphonies in order of composition while unpacking and arranging books and box files. Handling familiar things to familiar music made him feel so completely at home that he was surprised by rapping on his door and the hands of his clock pointing to midnight. He switched off the third movement of the *Pastoral* and opened the door saying quietly but emphatically, "I am very very very very –"

"Some people need sleep!" said a glaring young woman in dressing-gown and slippers.

"– very very sorry. I was so busy putting my things in order that I quite forgot the time and how sound can propagate through walls. Perhaps tomorrow – or some other day when you have a free moment – we can discover experimentally the greatest volume of sound I can produce without disturbing you, Miss . . . Miss?"

"Shutting your kitchen door will halve the din where we're concerned!" hissed the girl. "I'm surprised you haven't heard from the Jhas. He's up here complaining if we drop as much as a book on the floor."

She hurried away.

With a rueful grimace Mr Goodchild closed the door, crossed the room, closed the kitchen door and pondered a moment. He was not sleepy. The encounter with the young woman had pleasantly excited him. Sitting at his newly arranged work table he wound paper into what he thought of as "my trusty Remington" and, starting with the boarding-house address and date in the top right-hand corner, typed this.

My Very Dear Son,

You receive this communication at your work-place because I am no stranger to married life. If it arrived with other personal mail on your breakfast table Myra might feel hurt if you did not let her read it and equally hurt if you did. I must not offend either partner in a successful marital arrangement. My fortnight in Foxdene was a worthwhile

but unsuccessful experiment. It has proved
me too selfishly set in my ways to live without a room where I can work and eat according to my own timetable, a timetable which others cannot

He was interrupted by hesitant but insistent tapping and went to the door full of lively curiosity.

The young dressing-gowned woman outside was different from the previous one. He smiled kindly and asked, "How can I help you Miss . . ?"
"Thomson. Gwinny Thomson. My friend can't sleep because of the clattering your machine makes. Neither can I."
"To tell the truth Gwinny, when typing I get so engrossed in words that it's years since I noticed my machine made any noise at all. Your room-mate must be flaming mad with me."
Gwinny nodded once, hard.
"What's her name, Gwinny?"
"Karen Milton."
"Tell Karen that from now on my name is not George Goodchild but Mouse Goodchild. She won't hear a squeak from the kitchen tonight for I will go to bed with a small malt whisky instead of my usual cocoa and toasted cheese. But she must first endure the uproar of a flushing toilet if that sound also pierces your walls. Does it? And YOU must remember to call me George."
"We're used to the flushing so it doesn't bother us, Mr . . . George."
"Then Karen may now rest in peace. Good night, sleep tight Gwinny."

Gwinny retired. Mr Goodchild changed into slippers and pyjamas, took towel and toilet bag to bathroom, brushed teeth, washed, shat and smiled approvingly into the lavatory pan before flushing it. Sleek fat droppings showed that his inside still harmonized with the universe.

Next morning he arose, shaved, washed, dressed, breakfasted and waited until he heard the girls leave for work. Then he switched on the end of the *Pastoral* symphony, read the last six lines of his interrupted letter and completed it.

My fortnight in Foxdene was a worthwhile but unsuccessful experiment. It has proved me too selfishly set in my ways to live without a room where I can work and eat according to my own timetable, a timetable which others cannot be expected to tolerate.

This is my second day of boarding-house life and I am settling in nicely. My closest connections so far have been with Mrs Dewhurst our saturnine house-keeper, Mr Jha an excitable Asiatic shopkeeper, and two young secretaries in the room next door. Karen Milton is sexy and sure of herself and thinks I'm a boring old creep. No wonder! Gwinny Thomson is a sort teachers recognize at a glance: less attractive than her friend because less confident and needing someone she feels is stronger to hide behind. I'm afraid Karen bullies

her sometimes. Gwinny ought to "shack up"
(as the Americans say) with an experienced
man who thoroughly appreciates her, then
she might blossom. But I'm far too old for
that little job.

So have no fear, son o' mine. When I
kick the bucket all I have will be yours,
apart from £2500 for the UCF who will
probably spend half of it renovating a
Victorian drinking fountain on Ilkley
Moor and waste the rest attaching a bronze
plaque inscribed to my memory. I should
put a clause in my will forbidding such
wicked waste but there are uglier ways
to be remembered.

The Fellowship is forwarding my mail
here. A big stack arrived by first post
this morning so my editorial work with
the newsletter has not been interrupted.
The only upsetting thing here is the
pattern of the carpet. It looks fierce
enough to bite off any foot standing on
it. Give my love to Myra and the kids.
I will visit Foxdene for a couple of
days when she feels fit enough for a
short dose of me. Ask her to suggest a
weekend when I can babysit while you
take her out for "a night on the town".
Take care of yourself, son.

Mr Goodchild lifted his fountain pen from a small
glass tray of stamps and paperclips, pulled the letter
from the drum and wrote *Love from Dad* neatly at

the foot of it. A week later he typed this.

Dear, Dear Harry,

I have solved the problem of
the carpet by turning it upside down.
Through the weave of the brown backing
the jagged pattern looks faded, antique
and restful. When Mrs Dewhurst called
for the rent yesterday she stared at
the carpet, then at me. I smiled sweetly
back. She must think I'm daft.

I would have liked a reply to my last
letter because I've been feeling a bit
lonely and dreaming a lot about your
mother. She comes to me quite unlike
her usual self and accuses me of all
sorts of improbable crimes - dismantling
the British rail system was the worst.
A family man suddenly deprived of family
must feel low until new friendships fill
the gap and last night I had a surprising
social triumph.

Gwinny Thomson, probably acting under
orders from Karen, had come to me the
night before and said she and her friend
were going to have a party - not a rowdy
do, but there might be music and chat
till after midnight if I had no objection.
I said I had no objection to anything
which happened at their party as long as
I was invited. She was horrified but
tried to hide it by saying "of course" I

was invited. But I let the girls down gently by joining the party late after it had plenty of time to warm up. But it hadn't warmed up. The guests were all office workers in their twenties and early thirties, female colleagues of the girls and male colleagues of their boyfriends. They stood huddled in groups of three or four, talking in low voices and obviously waiting for the earliest possible moment to leave without seeming rude, while Karen served them drinks and tried without success to get them chatting and mingling. The source of embarrassment was Gwinny and her boyfriend, Tom. Gwinny was on the verge of tears. Tom kept turning his back and talking to other women whenever she came near.

Enter Mr Goodchild looking exactly like his name – small, stout, cheery and too innocent to notice anything wrong. This act of mine is not a phony one. Humanity would have become extinct centuries ago if what holds folk together were not stronger than what pulls us apart. My act worked. Folk clustered round me. The UCF also came in handy. Karen's boyfriend is an architect and thanks to the Fellowship urban conservation is a source of more profitable commissions than it was ten years ago. Karen's bloke asked such detailed questions about our projects

that I took him back to my room to show
him photographs. Karen was not pleased
about that and came too, so I sweetened
her by offering both of them a tot of
The Macallan. Then everyone but Gwinny
and Tom came here too so I set up the
epidiascope and gave my introductory
lecture on the renovation of Britain's
industrial heritage. You've never
attended my lectures, Harry, so don't
know that this one, though devised for
schoolchildren, draws bigger laughs from
adults. I got a round of applause which
brought the Dewhursts up from their
basement. Them too I sweetened with
nips of The Macallan. Lastly Tom and
Gwinny entered hand in hand, him
grinning as smugly as an office boy who
had just seduced a company director's
daughter, her as bashful as a bride on
her honeymoon. They had obviously been
reconciled by a bout of what the Scotch
call "hockmagandy" and the nasty lad
liked flaunting the fact more than poor
Gwinny did. I sent everyone away by
saying it was my bedtime.

I understand your silence, Harry.
Perhaps my stay at Foxdene would have
ended more kindly – or not ended at
all – if I had discussed my domestic
problem with you instead of Myra. We
might have found a solution she would
have accepted – like me buying a modern

Portakabin with all mod cons, one you
could have set up behind the big hedge
hiding the kitchen garden from the lawn.
Myra need never have seen me during
the day and I could have shared the
regular evening meals and Sunday lunch,
and helped the kids with their homework.
You and I could have enjoyed an
occasional game of chess like in the
old days and my music would have
irritated nobody. But you and I never
discuss things. It's my fault. When
you were little I always told you
everything I knew in such detail that
you recoiled into reticence like your
mother and, unlike your mother, never
told me to shut up. No wonder you won't
answer letters. But I will burble on
to you since I have nobody else.

I enclose bulldozer, roadroller and
pickup truck for Nigel's Dinky Toy
collection, and a set of Flower Fairy
books for Tracy.

Love from

Dad.

Exactly a week later Mr Goodchild started typing
his last letter in that boarding house.

Dear Harry,
When I came here a fortnight
back I told the housekeeper that nobody
over fifty can foretell how they'll be

living a few months hence. I was wrong.
A few days, a few hours hence would be
more accurate. I'll explain this.

On the evening of the day after the
party I accidentally passed Karen, then
Gwinny on our landing. The quick angry
manner of one and the glum look of the
other suggested a quarrel, though their
replies to my greeting showed it was
not with me. Later I heard a slamming
of doors then silence. Thinking both
had gone out I started playing
Mendelssohn's "Italian" symphony louder
than I've dared play anything since my
first night here. The rhythm was helping
me rattle through my report for our
annual general meeting when someone
tapped the door. Was this Mr Jha? Had
my long-lost son motored over from
Bracknell? It was Gwinny. I said,
"Sorry, I thought you were out, I'll
turn down the noise."
"I like that music – it's cheerful," said
she.
"Come in and listen," said I, "if you
can stand the noise of my typewriter
too."
She sat by the fire while I finished the
report, then I put on Vivaldi's "Seasons"
and made us a little snack. We consumed
it seated on opposite sides of the table
like a married couple. Suddenly she said,
"Karen's not the bad one. It's me who's

bad. I'm jealous of her lovely boyfriend
so I make scenes when she borrows my
hairbrush or leaves a crumby plate on
the mantelpiece."
I hate heartfelt confessions. I told
her I enjoyed the company of quiet folk
and sometimes liked the company of
talkative ones but complainers bored
me, especially if they complained about
themselves. She pulled a sour face at
that then suddenly cheered up and told
me horrible stories about her boyfriend
Tom, playing them for laughs. She's a
good little comedian so I laughed quite
a lot though I said not one word for or
against him. I told her I wanted to do
some reading now and if she decided to
stay she could play any of my tapes she
liked. That's how the rest of the evening
went. At half past ten I noticed her
listening for the return of Karen so
got rid of her by saying it was my
bedtime and we parted with expressions
of mutual esteem – I said she'd been as
good as a pussy cat. I tell you all
this, Harry, to show that I did not
invite what follows.

Last night noises from next door
suggested that once again the residents
were not in perfect harmony. At my usual
hour I went to bed with a mug of sweet
hot chocolate and J B Priestley's
history of the old northern music halls.

Around midnight the door softly opens and Gwinny creeps in, dressed for outdoors and with a finger to her lips. In a low voice she explains that horrible Tom had invited her to spend the night at his place, but when she got there he was so horrible that they'd quarrelled and split up, probably for good. Returning to her own room she found Karen in bed with <u>her</u> bloke who was obviously expecting to spend the night there. Gwinny, in no mood to explain her change of plan, pretended she'd come back for a toothbrush or something, grabbed it, went downstairs then realized she hadn't money for a hotel and a respectable bed-and-breakfast place would not want a girl without luggage. So here she was!

Without a word I got up, put two armchairs together and made them up as a bed using cushions, a quilt, a bedcover I do not need, and two overcoats. I told her that I would not be gentlemanly and give her my bed, because if I lay on the chairs my old bones would stop me from sleeping and force me to crawl in beside her. I offered to make her a cup of cocoa. She refused. I returned to bed and lay with my back to her while she undressed and lay down, then I put the light out.

But I was quite unable to sleep and

restless movements from her part of the
room showed neither could she. Sounds
from the room next door were to blame.
After an hour or two she heaved a great
sigh and began talking about her family
and Karen and Tom. I think most of it
was complaints but her low monotonous
voice worked like a lullaby. I kept
muttering "I see" and "that's a pity"
between moments of dozing off. At last
she said something complicated which I
asked her to repeat: "I'm afraid I'm
developing a father-fixation on you."
I said she shouldn't use Freud's
vocabulary when she'd never read him.
She said, "You're right. Why must you
always be right? You're giving me an
inferiority complex."
I told her that now she was quoting
Adler and that before Adler described
the inferiority complex folk just said
they felt shy. For a while we lay
listening to the faint sounds of Karen
gasping and her architect grunting in
unison. I had forgotten to shut the
kitchen door. I was about to ask Gwinny
to shut it because she was nearer when
she asked in a tiny voice if I'd like
her to join me in bed. I said I would.
Nothing much came of it but enough for
us to fall comfortably asleep together
afterwards. We slept sound till nearly
ten in the morning.

Over the breakfast table (usual

English breakfast) she apologized for being bad at lovemaking. I asked why she thought she was. She said Tom had said so. I asked how often they had made love. After a lot of hesitation she said once, on the night of the party. I chuckled at that and said all she needed was some more lovemaking with someone she did not think horrible. She stared at me then said, "Are you asking me to ..?" and went on staring without another word. I said cheerily, "Nay! At my age I can ask nothing from lovely young women but I can't stop hoping. I'm a great hoper."

I felt young, Harry. Twenty years younger at least. I still do. Is that stupid of me?

Suddenly she laughed and jumped up saying, "I don't care if those two next door ARE still in bed, it's my room as much as Karen's and I'm going in, see you later George."

She grabbed her things and rushed out. That was forty minutes ago. Now just suppose, Harry,

Mr Goodchild stopped typing and thought hard, then went to the kitchen and made a cup of camomile tea. From the next room came sounds of two women and a man exchanging casual, friendly words. Once Gwinny said something and the others laughed. Mr Goodchild sat before his typewriter again and stared at the unfinished letter until someone forcefully knocked on his door. Mrs Dewhurst stood outside. She said, "A visitor for you," and went away. Her place was taken by a big man wearing a business suit.

"So the mountain has come to Mahomet! Come in," said Mr Goodchild pleasantly. "Would you like a cup of tea? Have a seat."

The big man entered but did not sit. His mouth and eyes resembled Mr Goodchild's but their expression was careworn. Glancing round the room he asked, "How are you, Dad?"

"Never better. How's the garage?"

"Listen, Dad, I've talked to Myra about your Portakabin notion. She agrees to it."

"That's interesting but there's no need for haste, Harry. Let her think it over for a month or two. How's Nigel and Tracy?"

"They keep asking for you. Come back to us. Do it today."

"Don't be daft, Harry! It'll take months for you to get planning department permission for a cabin in your vegetable patch, no matter how many palms you grease. I asked how the garage is doing."

"It needs me there as much as it always does!" said his son impatiently. "A small businessman can't afford days off and I'm not going to stand here gassing. Myra says you shall have your shelf in the fridge and make your own lunches till the Portakabin comes."

"Anything else?" said Mr Goodchild, staring hard at him.

"You can also use our guest room as a work room."

"Where will your guests sleep, Harry?"

"On the bed settee in the living-room," said Harry, sighing.

"At last, my son, you are talking sense. Shake!" said Mr Goodchild holding out his hand. His son shook it a little wearily but with obvious relief, then left after another minute of conversation.

Mr Goodchild walked to his typewriter and stared at the single sheet of paper typed closely on both sides. After a moment he pulled it out, tore it carefully into small bits and dropped them in a waste basket. He then entered the kitchen, put four glasses on a tray, poured a small measure of The Macallan into each and placed the tray on his work table. Then he left the room, opened the door of the room next door and stuck his head round it without knocking. Karen, Karen's architect and Gwinny sat with mugs in their hands, staring at him.

"Boo!" he said. "You must all come into my place – now – this instant. I have something to celebrate and can't do it alone. Leave those mugs! Drink will be provided."

He returned to his room. They filed in after him, Gwinny looking as curious and willing to be pleased as the others but slightly apprehensive. He gave her a reassuring nod as he handed round the whisky glasses. Glass in hand he then faced the three of them, proposed a toast to family affection, clinked his glass with theirs and took off the contents of his own in one swallow. As they sipped theirs he told them of Harry's visit and what he had said.

". . . which brings my stay here to a satisfying conclusion. Of course I knew before I came he would want me back. I just didn't know when. Now YOU! –" (he told Karen's architect) "– have a car. Right?"

The architect nodded.

"Half an hour from now you must drive us to the best restaurant you know where I will order and pay for a slap-up celebration champagne lunch. Of course the driver won't be allowed more than a couple of glasses. But this is not an unselfish proposal. Afterwards you must help me pack my things because a van will arrive this evening to take me and them back to Bracknell."

Gwinny said, "I'm not coming. I'm expecting a phone call from Tom."

She put down her glass and left the room so abruptly that she left a silence.

Mr Goodchild looked enquiringly at his two remaining guests. After a moment Karen said apologetically, "She used to be quite a sensible girl – I would never have shared a room with her if she'd always been so moody. I thought it was Tom who upset her but an hour ago she came home from a night with him so cheerful and relaxed I thought he'd done her some good for a change. She was chatting quite happily before we came in here. I'll never understand her now. Maybe it's my fault."

The kitchen door was open and from the room next door they heard faint sounds of sobbing. Mr Goodchild drowned them by talking in a more Yorkshire accent than he normally used.

"Nay lass, you aren't the world's conscience! You can help some people sometimes but nobody all the time – that's my philosophy. Let's go for that lunch I promised you."

MONEY

IN BRITAIN ONLY snobs, perverts and the wholly despairing want friendship with richer or poorer folk. Maybe in Iceland or Holland or Canada factory-owners and labourers, lumber-jacks and high court judges eat in each other's houses and go holidays together. If so they must have equally good food, clothes and schools for their children. That kind of classlessness is impossible here. Mackay disagrees. He says the Scots have democratic traditions which let them forget social differences. He says his father was gardener to a big house in the north and the owner was his dad's best friend. On rainy days they sat in the gardener's shed and drank a bottle of whisky together. But equal incomes allow steadier friendships than equal drunkenness. I did not want to borrow money from Mackay because it proved I was poorer than him. He insisted on lending, which ruined more than our friendship.

I needed a thousand pounds cash to complete a

piece of business and phoned my bank to arrange
a loan. They said I could have it at an interest of
eleven per cent plus a forty-pound arrangement fee.
I told them I would repay in five days but they said
that made no difference – for £1000 now I must
repay £1150, even if I did so tomorrow. I groaned,
said I would call for the money in half an hour, put
down the phone and saw Mackay. He had strolled
in from his office next door. We did the same sort
of work but were not competitors. When I got more
business than I could handle I passed it to him, and
vice versa.

He said, "What have you to groan about?"
I told him and added, "I can easily pay eleven per
cent et cetera but I hate it. I belong to the financial
past. I agree with Maynard Keynes – all interest
above five per cent strikes me as extortion."
"I'll lend you a thousand, interest free," said Mackay
pulling out his cheque book. While I explained why I
never borrow money from friends he filled in a cheque,
tore it off and held it out saying, "Stop raving about
equality and take this to my bank. I'll phone them and
they'll cash it at once. We're still equals – in an
emergency you would do the same for me."
I blushed because he was almost certainly wrong. Then
I shrugged, took the cheque and said, "If this is what
you want, Mackay, all right. Fine. I'll return it within
five days, or within a fortnight at most."
"Harry, I know that. Don't worry," said Mackay
soothingly and started talking about something else. I
felt grateful but angry because I hate feeling grateful. I

also hated his easy assumption that his money was perfectly safe. Had I lent *him* a thousand pounds I would have worried myself sick until I got it back. If being aristocratic means preferring good manners to money then Mackay was definitely posher than me. Did he think his dad's boozing sessions with Lord Glenbannock had *ennobled* the Mackays? The loan was already spoiling our friendship.

Five days later my business was triumphantly concluded and I added a cheque for over ten thousand pounds to my bank account. I was strongly tempted *not* to repay Mackay at once just to show him I was something more dangerous than decent, honest, dependable old Harry. I stayed honest longer by remembering that if I repaid promptly I would be able to borrow from him again on the same convenient terms. Since handing him a cheque would have been as embarrassing as taking one I decided to put the cash straight back into his bank. Despite computerization my bank would have taken two or three days to transfer the money, which would have meant Mackay getting it back the following week. I collected ten crisp new hundred-pound notes in a smooth envelope, placed envelope in inner jacket pocket and walked the half mile to Mackay's bank. The morning air was mild but fresh, the sky one sheet of high grey cloud which threatened rain but might hold off till nightfall.

Mackay's bank is reached by a road where I lived when I was married. I seldom go there now. On one side buildings have been demolished and replaced by

a cutting holding a six-lane motorway. Tenements
and shops on the other side no longer have a thriving
look. I was walking carefully along the cracked and
pitted pavement when I heard a woman say, "Harry!
What are *you* doing here?"
She was thin, sprightly, short-haired and (like most
attractive women nowadays) struck me as any age
between sixteen and forty. I said I was going to a bank
to repay money I owed and ended by asking, "How
are your folk up at Ardnamurchan, Liz?"
She laughed and said, "I'm *Mish* you idiot! Come inside
– Wee Dougie and Davenport and Roy and Roberta
are there and we haven't seen you for ages."
I remembered none of these names but never say no
to women who want me. I followed her into the
Whangie, though it was not a pub I liked. The
Whangie's customers may not have been prone to
violence but its drab appearance had always made me
think they were, so the pleasure I felt at the sight of the
dusty brown interior was wholly unexpected. It was
exactly as it had been twenty or thirty years before,
exactly like most Scottish pubs before the big breweries
used extravagant tax reliefs to buy them up and
decorate them like Old English taverns or Spanish
bistros. The only wall decorations were still solidly
framed mirrors frosted with the names and emblems
of defunct whisky blends. This was still a dour Scottish
drinking-den which kept the prices down by spending
nothing on appearance, and it was nearly empty, being
soon after opening-time. Crying, "Look who's here!"
Mish led me to people round a corner table, one of
whom I knew. He said, "Let me get you a drink Harry,"

starting to stand, but, "No no no sit down sit down,"
I said and hurried to the bar. Apart from the envelope
in my inner jacket pocket I had just enough cash to
buy a half pint of lager. I carried this back to the
people in the corner. They made room for me.

A fashion note. None of us looked smart. The others
wore jeans with shapeless denim or leather jackets, I
wore my old tweed jacket and crumpled corduroys.
Only my age marked me off from the rest, I thought,
and not much. The man I knew, a musician called Roy,
was almost my age. The one oddity among us was the
not-Mish woman, Roberta. Her hair was the colour of
dry straw and stood straight upright on top of her skull,
being clipped or shaved to thin stubble at the back
and sides. The wing of her right nostril was pierced by
several fine little silver rings. Her lipstick was dull purple.
She affected me like someone with a facial deformity
so to avoid staring hard I completely ignored her. This
was easy as she never said a word the whole time I was
in the Whangie. She seemed depressed about
something. When others spoke to her she answered
by sighing or grunting or shrugging her shoulders.

First they asked how I was getting on and I answered,
"Not bad – not good." The truth was that like many
professional folk nowadays I am doing extremely well
even though I sometimes have to borrow money. It
would have been unkind to tell them how much better
off I was because they were obviously unemployed.
Why else did they drink, and drink very slowly, at half
past eleven on Thursday morning? I avoided distressing

topics by talking to Roy, the musician. We had met at a party where he sang and played the fiddle really well. Since then I had seen him busking in the shopping precincts and had passed quickly on the other side of the street to avoid embarrassing him, for he was too good a musician to be living that way. I asked him about the people who had held the party, not having seen them since. Neither had Roy so we discussed the party. Ten minutes later we had nothing more to say about it and I had drunk my half pint. I stood up and said, "Have to go now folks."

They fell silent and looked at me. I felt that they expected something, and blushed, and spoke carefully to avoid stammering: "You see, I would like to buy a round before I go but I've no cash on me. I mean, I've plenty of money in my bank – and I have my cheque book here – could one of you cash a cheque for five pounds? – I promise it won't stot."

Nobody answered. I realized nobody there had five pounds on them or the means of turning my cheque into cash if they had.

"Cash it at the bar Harry," said Mish.

"I would like to – but do you think the barman will do it without a cheque card?"

"No cheque card?" said Mish on a shrill note.

"None! I've never had a cheque card. If I had I would lose it. I'm always losing things. But the barmen in Tennent's cash my cheques without one . . ."

Davenport, who had a black beard and a firm manner, waved to the barman and said, "Jimmy, this pal of ours wants to cash a cheque. He's Harry Haines, a well-known character in the west end with a good going business –"

"In fact he's loaded," said Mish –

"– and you would oblige us by cashing a cheque for him. He's left his cheque card at home."

"Sorry," said the barman, "there's nothing I can do about that."

He turned his back on us.

"I'm sorry too," I told them helplessly.

"You," Mish told me, "are a mean old fart. You are not only mean, you are a bore. You are totally uninteresting."

At these my words my embarrassment vanished and I cheered up. I no longer minded my social superiority. I felt boosted by it. With an air of mock sadness I said, "True! So I must leave you. Goodbye folks."

I think the three men were also amused by the turn things had taken. They said cheerio to me quite pleasantly.

I left the Whangie and went toward Mackay's bank, carefully remembering the previous ten minutes to see if I might have done better with them. I did not regret entering the Whangie with Mish. She had pleasantly excited me and I had not then known she only saw me as a source of free drink. True, I had talked boringly – had bored myself as well as them – but interesting topics would have emphasized the social gulf between us. I might have amused them with queer stories about celebrities whose private lives are more open to me than to popular journalism (that was probably how the duke entertained Mackay's father between drams in the tool shed) but it strikes me as an unpleasant way to cadge favour with underlings. I was pleased to think I had

been no worse than a ten-minute bore. I had made
a fool of myself by wanting credit for a round of drinks
I did not buy, but that kind of foolery hurts nobody. If
Mish and her pals despised me for it good luck to
them. I did not despise myself for it, or only slightly.
In the unexpected circumstances I was sure I could
not have behaved better.

The idea of taking a hundred-pound note from
Mackay's money and buying a round of drinks only
came to me later. So did the idea of handing the note
to Mish, saying, "Share this with the others," and
leaving fast before she could reply. So did the best
idea of all: I could have laid five hundred-pound notes
on the table, said, "Conscience money, a hundred
each," and hurried off to put the rest in Mackay's
account. Later I could have told him, "I paid back
half what I owe today. You'll have to wait till next
week for the rest – I've done something stupid with
it." As he heard the details his mouth would open
wider and wider or his frown grow sterner and sterner.
At last he would say, "That's the last interest-free
loan you get from me" – or something else. But he
would have been as astonished as the five in the
pub. I would have proved I was not predictable.
Behaving like that would have changed me for the
better. But I could not imagine doing such things then.
I can only imagine them since I changed for the worse.

I walked from the Whangie toward Mackay's bank
brooding on my recent adventure. No doubt there
was a smug little smile on my lips. Then I noticed

someone walking beside me and a low voice saying, "Wait a minute."

I stopped. My companion was Roberta who stood staring at me. She was breathing hard, perhaps with the effort of overtaking me, and her mouth was set in something like a sneer. I could not help looking straight at her now. Everything I saw – weird hair and sneering face, shapeless leather jacket with hands thrust into flaps below her breasts, baggy grey jeans turned up at the bottoms to show clumsy thick-soled boots laced high up the ankles – all these insulted my notion of how a woman ought to look. But her alert stillness as her breathing quietened made me feel very strange, as if I had seen her years ago, and often. To break the strangeness I said sharply, "Well?"

Awkwardly and huskily she said, "I don't think you're mean or uninteresting. I like older men."

Her eyes were so wide open that I saw the whole circle of the pupils, one brown, one blue. There was a kind of buzzing in my blood and the nearby traffic sounded fainter. I felt stronger and more alive than I had felt for years – alive in a way I had never expected to feel again after my marriage went wrong. Her sneer was now less definite, perhaps because I felt it on my own lips. Yes, I was leering at her like a gangster confronting his moll in a 1940 cinema poster and she was staring back as if terrified to look anywhere else. I was fascinated by the thin stubble at the sides of her head above the ears. It must feel exactly like my chin before I shaved in the morning. I wanted to rub it hard with the palms of my hands. I heard myself say, "You want money. How?"

She murmured that I could visit my bank before we went to her place – or afterward, if I preferred. My leer became a wide grin. I patted my inner pocket and said, "No need for a bank, honey. I got everything you want right here. And we'll take a taxi to my place, not yours."
I spoke with an American accent, and the day turned into one of the worst in my life.

EDISON'S
TRACTATUS

PERHAPS YOU KNOW that musclemen – hard men who want to be extra strong – have a habit of eating big feeds of steak and chips, and the minute the last mouthful is swallowed they heave big weights, or run great distances, or work machines that let them do both at the same time. This converts all the food in their guts into muscle without an ounce of additional fat. When a dedicated muscleman overeats, sheer strength is the only outcome.

There was once a man who trained that way to strengthen his brain. Not only after but *during* big feeds he would read very deep books – trigonometry, accountancy, divinity, that class of subject – and think about them fiercely and continually till he felt hungry again. He grew so brainy that before you said a word to him he guessed the sort of thing you meant to say and quoted Jesus or Euclid or Shakespeare who had said it better. This destroyed his social life but at first he didn't care.

One day he was sitting in a restaurant reading Edison's *Tractatus* and beasting into his third plate of steak and chips when he noticed a young woman across the table from him eating the same stuff. She had cut it into small bits and was forking them steadily into her mouth with one hand while writing just as steadily with the other. She wrote in red ink on a block of the squared paper scientists use for charts and diagrams, but she was writing words as clear as print, words so neat and regular that he could not stop staring at them although they were illegible from where he sat being upside down. He noticed that the woman, though not a small woman, was neat and regular in a way that suggested a school mistress. He could not imagine what she would say if she spoke to him and the strangeness of this put him in a confusion through which at last he heard his voice ask if she would please pass the salt cellar, which was as close to him as to her.

The woman glanced at the salt cellar – at him – smiled – put her fork down and said, "What will I most dislike about you if I let that request lead to intimate friendship?"
He hesitated then said frankly, "My breadth of knowledge. I talk better about more things than anyone else. Nobody likes me for it."
She nodded and said, "What do you know about the interface between pre-Columbian Aztec pottery, Chinese obstetrics during the Ming dynasty and the redrawing of constituency boundaries in the Lothian Region subsequent to the last general election?"
He said, "They are perfect examples of inter-disciplinary

cross-sterilization. When William Blake said that *The dog starved at his master's gate predicts the ruin of the state* he was stating a political fact. The writer who traced a North American hurricane back to a butterfly stamping on a leaf in a tropical rain forest was reasoning mathematically. The absurd interface you posit is (like most post-modernist and post-constructionalist concepts) a sort of mental afterbirth. Are you writing about it?"

"No but you can reach for the salt cellar yourself," she said and went on writing. The man felt a pang of unintelligent grief. He tried to quench it with manly anger. "Tell me just one thing!" he said sternly. "If we had conversed intimately what would I have most disliked about you?"

"My depth of sympathy," she answered with a patient sigh. "No matter how loud-mouthed, boastful and dismissive you grew I would realize you could never be different."

"O thank *God* you never passed me that salt cellar!" he cried.

And continued reading Edison's *Tractatus*
but could no longer concentrate.

EPILOGUE TO EDISON'S *TRACTATUS*

In 1960 I went on holiday to Ireland with Andrew Sykes, a tough small stocky man with a thick thatch of white hair and a face like a boxer's. Like myself he dressed comfortably rather than smartly. We had met when he was a mature student at Glasgow University and I a very callow one just out of Glasgow Art School.

We were from the working class who had benefited when two post-war governments (Labour and Tory) agreed that all who qualified for professional educations might have them whether or not they or their parents could pay. Andrew, who had been a sergeant with the British army in India, eventually won a doctorate through a paper on trade unions in the building industry, getting his knowledge by the unacademic ploy of working as a navvy. His army experience and a course in economics had also given him insights into the workings of our officer and financial class. He took malicious glee in gossiping to me about the insider trading by which this minority manipulate the rest. My notion of Britain had been formed at the end of the Second World War when our government announced the coming of a fairer society and the creation of social welfare for all. I had thought Britain was now mainly managed by folk who had mastered difficult processes through training and experience. Andrew explained that, as often today as in the past, most British civil service and business chiefs had stepped into senior positions because they had been to three or four expensive boarding schools and a couple of universities in the English east midlands: institutions where exams mattered less than their parents' wealth and friends they had made. He persuaded me that Britain was not (as most of our politicians and publicity networks claimed) a democracy, but an electoral aristocracy.

I thought Andrew disliked this unfair system since he was entering a profession through a socialist act of parliament. On our Irish holiday (we were guests of his friends Greta and David Hodgins at Nenagh in Tipperary) I was surprised to find he hated almost any group who wanted to change the dominant system. He even hated the Campaign for Nuclear Disarmament. He forgave me for being a member but we could not discuss it. The only political hope we shared was a wish for Scottish self-government. I enjoyed what I saw of Ireland but enjoyed his company less than I had expected. His hobbies were wrestling and judo. He told me that body builders convert steak into muscle by a course of weight-lifting immediately after a meal. I will say more about him because he gave me more than the first sentence of "Edison's *Tractatus*".

He became Strathclyde University's first Professor of Sociology in 1967, retired in 1989, died in 1991. His closest relatives were aunts with whom he lodged in a Glasgow tenement until they died long before he did. His job gave him prestige and colleagues. His holidays with the Hodgins in Tipperary gave him a family whose children regarded him as an uncle, a community which treated him as an equal. From a Labour Party member he became a xenophobic Tory. In the university staff club he once aimed a judo kick at a black visitor who was quietly minding his own business. Since his special study was trade unions in the 1980s he became a salaried adviser of the British government, telling Margaret Thatcher how to weaken them. He took self-conscious glee in the bowler hat, tailor-made striped trousers, black jacket and waistcoat he acquired for visits to Downing Street. I fear he did a lot of harm but not to me. From 1961 to 1974 he was my only steady patron. He bought paintings and lent money when I was in need, usually taking a drawing as repayment. He lent me money as if it was an ordinary, unimportant action, leaving my self-respect undamaged. I cannot type so he got his secretaries to type my poems, plays and first novel onto wax stencils from which (in days when photocopying was hugely expensive) they printed all the copies I needed without charge. In 1974 he arranged for the Collins Gallery of Strathclyde University to give the largest retrospective show my pictures have ever had, getting a Glasgow Lord Provost to open it.

Yet in his last fifteen years I hardly saw him at all, maybe because I no longer supported a family so had less need to borrow. After his retirement he became a recluse and solitary drinker, his only human contacts being a cleaning lady and a weekly phone call from Greta Hodgins in Ireland. I felt sad and guilty when he died. He had given me much more than I ever gave him.

I will now list other ingredients which went into "Edison's *Tractatus*".

1 In the 1960s I heard that Wittgenstein's *Tractatus* was a very brainy book. I thought it might not be too brainy for me but never got hold of a copy.

2 I am too shy and pessimistic to start conversations with strangers but when public transport or an eating house places me beside an attractive one I sometimes fantasize about talking to them. This habit led to my first television play and a novel which is still in print. In 1982 I worked with Liz Lochhead, Jim Kelman and Tom Leonard on a review called *The Pie of Damocles*. I scribbled a sketch in which a young woman at a café table asks a depressed young man to pass her the sugar bowl and he insists on discussing what this might lead to before refusing. My friends did not think it funny. I discarded it.

3 I started hearing the word *interface* in the 1970s. It seemed to be used by people erecting a barrier round their work practice while talking across it. The barrier made the job they had mastered feel safer but conversation across it sometimes made new work, as forensic medicine had developed from the interface between policing and doctoring. My facetious attitude to new words led me to link activities between which no interface was possible – the gap between Aztec pottery and Chinese obstetrics, for instance, seemed unbridgeable. Around the same time I heard a lecturer amuse a university audience by referring to something as "an example of interdisciplinary cross-sterilization".

4 For several years I have been perplexed by the adjective *post-modern*, especially when applied to my own writing, but have now decided it is an academic substitute for *contemporary* or *fashionable*. Its prefix honestly announces it as a specimen of intellectual

afterbirth, a fact I only noticed when I reread my brainy
character saying so.

5 A few years ago I heard that a scientist had shown
how a butterfly stamping on a leaf in a tropical rain
forest might precipitate a hurricane in North America.
This may or may not be true.

6 In the first months of 1994 I conducted a creative
writing class at St Andrews University. Going home by
train to Glasgow one day I sat opposite a young woman
who was writing in red ink on a block of graph paper. I
could not read her words but they were shaped with
unusual clearness and regularity. She was slightly bigger
than average, neatly dressed and with no apparent
make-up or anything to catch the eye. I felt a strong
prejudice in her favour, believing, perhaps wrongly, that
she was unusually intelligent. I suddenly wanted to put
her in a story exactly as she appeared. She sometimes
exchanged words with a young man beside her but
their conversation did not interest me.

I broke my journey home at Markinch to visit
Malcolm Hood in Glenrothes Hospital. Two years earlier
he had been paralysed by a cerebral stroke: his brain
was in full working order but his body could give no
sign of it. He was now able to speak and move a little.
On this visit I read him a story from Somerville and
Ross's *Experiences of an Irish R.M.* and occasional
comments and snorts of laughter showed his
enjoyment. When students at Glasgow Art School forty
years before we had often read aloud to each other

from amusing authors. My favourites were Max Beerbohm and Rabelais, Malcolm's were Dickens and Patrick Campbell. Campbell – an Anglo-Irish humorist not much read now – probably gave us our first taste of Blarney, which I define as *the employment of an Irish idiom to make an unlikely story more convincing.* The Somerville and Ross tale was full of it.

When I boarded a homeward-bound train at Markinch "Edison's *Tractatus*" was germinating. I scribbled most of it in a notebook before reaching Glasgow, and as I did so imagined an Irish voice saying it, an Irish voice deliberately constructing an improbable tale. That is why I gave it an improbable title. Were I to read it aloud I would do so in my Scottish voice, but when writing "Edison's *Tractatus*" the sentences moved to a second-hand Irish lilt.

7 This lilt must come from more than a fortnight in Tipperary thirty-five years ago and from renewed pleasure in the Blarney of Somerville and Ross. Flann O'Brien's writings are an ingredient because, though Joyce, Synge and O'Casey use Blarney on occasions, O'Brien is the only Irish genius whose work is Blarney throughout. In the previous six months I had also read with pleasure "This Fella I Knew", a short story by my friend Bernard MacLaverty who never talks Blarney and hardly ever writes it. This one story is an exception. It appears in his anthology, *Walking the Dog*, published in 1994.

8 A week after scribbling the first version of "Edison's *Tractatus*" a student in my St Andrews class asked how

I got ideas for stories. I gave a long confused answer
because each novel, short story or play seemed to
form differently. What set it going might be a story I
had read which I wanted to tell differently, or a day-
dream, or dream remembered on waking, or a fantasy
I had evolved during conversation, or an incident
which had befallen someone else but was
unforgettable because of its oddity, humour or
injustice. Ideas have sometimes come from
commissions to write on a particular subject.
Thereafter the idea grew through an alternation of
writing and deliberate day-dreaming. If a narrative
drew in many memories, ideas and phrases which
had lain unused in my brain it sometimes expanded
to a novella, novel or play. All but my first novel came
that way. The first came from childhood faith in a long
printed story as my surest way of getting attention. I
day-dreamed and scribbled it for years before
accumulating enough ideas and experiences to finish
it. I have also developed stories by telling or reading
parts to friends before completion. Most authors I
know avoid this because displaying unfinished work
reduces their enthusiasm for it, but some listeners'
suggestions have expanded my tales in ways I might
not have discovered by myself.

The student's question produced this account of
what went into "Edison's *Tractatus*". There is probably
more than I am conscious of, but I believe the brainy
hero is mainly a caricature of traits which Andrew Sykes
and I had in common. We were both inclined to turn
sexual urges into clever, sometimes boring monologues.

The urge to deliver an uninterrupted monologue is the energy driving most teachers, story-tellers and politicians. "Edison's *Tractatus*" is obviously a portrait of someone too wordy for his own good, which also explains the addition of this bit of intellectual afterbirth.

THE SHORTEST
TALE

MOST BOOKS NOWADAYS are made of big paper sheets printed, folded and cut into units of thirty-two pages, units which bookbinders call *signatures*. This book contains five signatures – exactly 160 pages. Since the first five stories do not quite fill them I will write another, a true one because just now my imagination can invent nothing short enough. Like other stories in this book it deals with education. I heard it from Angela Mullane, once a colleague of the teacher who is the story's most active yet least interesting character.

A school in the east of Glasgow taught children who could barely read, or found it hard to sit still and concentrate, or had other traits which unsuited them for normal schooling without qualifying them for medical care. In times of full employment (and this was in a time of full employment) such children can be prepared for ordinary jobs by teaching them to read, count and talk with greater confidence, but they cannot be taught really well in classes of more than ten. The average class size was twenty-five so the teachers often had to teach badly. Before 1986 this meant threatening and sometimes inflicting physical pain. Deliberately inflicted pain was in those days used by teachers in schools for normally healthy and even wealthy children – why should the damaged children of poor folk suffer less?

The pupils mostly came from a council housing scheme built for the very poor in the early 1930s. People there felt that the police were more of a threat than a protection, so small weak people believed that a strong male member of their own family was their likeliest defender. In many Scottish schools the most effective-sounding threat a pupil could hurl at a punitive teacher was, "I'll get my dad to you!" This threat was almost a ritual. Teachers had a stock of equally ritualized replies to it. But many children in the school I speak of had no father or uncle or big brother in their family, and knew that their teachers knew it. A few had mothers with dogs, perhaps for protection. These were able to say, "I'll get my dug to you."

One day at this school a small boy faced a teacher wielding a leather belt designed for striking people. The boy was either trying to stop himself being beaten or had been beaten already and wished to show he was not completely crushed. Either in fear of pain or in a painful effort to keep some dignity he cried out, "I'll get my –" and hesitated, then cried, "I'll get my

Alstation to you!" He lived with a granny who could not afford to keep a big dog. The way he pronounced Alsatian proved that his dog was nothing but a badly learned word – a word without power – a word which got him laughed at.

This happened in 1971 or 72 when public education and health were better funded, when British manual workers were better paid, when the middle classes were almost as prosperous but less in debt than today, when the richest classes were (by their own obviously high standards) much poorer.
Other tales in this book have sour endings
but none as bad as this because
the others are fiction.

Glasgow, 20th December 1995

GOODBYE

INDEPENDENCE